The door of Lord Barton's cabin opened with a bang.

Four young men staggered in, led by the young gentlemen whom Barton had snubbed so throroughly on deck.

Barton groaned and leapt from the bunk. He tried in vain to position himself so that Amanda was invisible to the intruders.

"I say, Barton, I think you owe me an—" The young man stopped, and his eyes widened. "Be damned!" he said.

The other gentlemen, too, stopped dead at the sight of Barton and Amanda.

"Well, I like that!" the first young man exclaimed. "He gives me the cut direct, as if he weren't down here frolicking with a prime bit himself."

Amanda sat frozen, her hands clasped to her pale cheeks.

Barton thought of Amanda's grandfather and all that he had meant to him. With a feeling of total helplessness he rose to his feet. "You appear to be labouring under a misapprehension, gentlemen," he said coldly. He took Amanda's icy hand in his own. "Allow me to present my future wife."

Regency England: 1811-1820

"It was the best of times,
it was the worst of times...."

As George III languished in madness, the pampered and profligate Prince of Wales led the land in revelry and the elegant Beau Brummel set the style. Across the Channel, Napoleon continued to plot against the English until his final exile to St. Helena. Across the Atlantic, America renewed hostilities with an old adversary, declaring war on Britain in 1812. At home, Society glittered, love matches abounded and poets such as Lord Byron flourished. It was a time of heroes and villains, a time of unrelenting charm and gaiety, when entire fortunes were won or lost on a turn of the dice and reputation was all. A dazzling period that left its mark on two continents and whose very name became a byword for elegance and romance.

Books by Elizabeth Michaels

HARLEQUIN REGENCY ROMANCE
17—TOLLIN'S DAUGHTER
58—THE FABRIC OF LOVE
83—THE CYNIC

Don't miss any of our special offers. Write to us at the following address for information on our newest releases.

Harlequin Reader Service
P.O. Box 1397, Buffalo, NY 14240
Canadian address: P.O. Box 603,
Fort Erie, Ont. L2A 5X3

LORD BARTON'S HONOUR

Elizabeth Michaels

Harlequin Books

TORONTO • NEW YORK • LONDON
AMSTERDAM • PARIS • SYDNEY • HAMBURG
STOCKHOLM • ATHENS • TOKYO • MILAN
MADRID • WARSAW • BUDAPEST • AUCKLAND

Published July 1993

ISBN 0-373-31201-6

LORD BARTON'S HONOUR

CHAPTER ONE

CHARLES WENDOVER hunched his thin shoulders against the cold wind that blew off the water, and shivered as he looked up at the dark clouds scurrying across the sky. "Why the devil must we leave today?" he grumbled. The ship *Cumberland Rover* rolled against the French dock, and the tall, lanky young man regained his balance with a curse. "Dashed muddy-looking day for crossing the Channel."

His companion shrugged. "I want to be back in England for quarter day," William, Lord Barton said. "I have tenants to see." He leaned lightly against the rail of the ship, his curly-brimmed beaver hat pulled low on his brow. Barton was not much above the average in height, but his trim figure and broad shoulders bespoke the sportsman. Dark hair curled over the collar of his greatcoat; his eyes, when he glanced at his friend Wendover, were a bright blue. "I dare say you will survive the trip."

"Your grandmother won't mind seeing to everything if you're not back in time," Charles Wendover persisted. "After seven weeks away, surely we can wait one more day before leaving."

"We have already waited three days for the weather to conform to your overly nice requirements," Barton said. "I'll be damned if I'll wait any longer."

"I call it cruel of you, Bart," Chas said. "After dragging me over to France in the first place..."

"I didn't 'drag' you over, Chas," Lord Barton said. "You told me you were damned tired of England in February and would welcome a change."

"After dragging me to France in the first place," Chas Wendover continued inexorably, "you insist on my returning home in this cursed weather." He looked at the sky again and shuddered.

"Seasickness is not fatal, you know, Chas," Barton said with a chuckle.

"No, it's worse than fatal," Chas said. "One can only wish in vain that one would die!" He huddled against the rail of the ship, his voluminous cloak pulled tight around his body.

"I feel certain that your constitution is equal to the strain," Barton drawled. "It will pass as soon as you are back on dry land."

"How terribly compassionate of you," Chas said gloomily. "You would receive your just deserts if I were to die on you, right in the middle of the Channel."

"I shall chance it," his friend said drily. Barton pushed himself away from the rail. "Let's go and find the captain," he said. "I want to see how much longer it will be before we cast off."

As he followed his friend across the deck, Chas glanced up at Barton. "I would never have thought to see you so anxious to return home," he said slyly.

"You seemed in enough of a hurry to leave. Recovered so soon from your fear of la Travers?"

Barton grunted irritably. "I was never afraid of Carolyn Travers," he said. "It only seemed..."

"Prudent?" supplied Chas, grinning.

"Prudent," Barton agreed wryly. "She needed a little time to cool off. To be given one's *congé* is never pleasant."

"Along with an expensive parting gift, I have no doubt?" Chas said.

Barton grimaced. "Emeralds," he said. "Rather a lot of them!"

"A wise choice," Chas said. "A magnificent woman, Carolyn, but rather a handful—those green-eyed females always are. I was rather surprised that you took up with her in the first place, to tell you the truth. Generally, you seem to prefer a more restful type of female."

Barton shrugged. "Dare I say that I was rather flattered by her determined pursuit of me?"

"That cannot be such a novelty for you," Chas said. "Why, every unmarried young lady in London, and every ambitious mama, has set her cap for you. Comes of possessing such a fortune, of course. Surely being pursued has lost its appeal?"

"Lord, yes," Barton said. "But being pursued by a woman like Carolyn Travers is a startling change from being chased by some milk-and-water miss intent on catching a husband."

"I wonder," Chas said musingly.

"Wonder what?" Barton asked.

"I've often thought," Chas said, "that Carolyn might have had hopes of becoming Lady Barton."

"Don't be ridiculous," Barton scoffed. "A woman of Carolyn's experience knows the ways of the world. Dash it all, a man don't marry his mistress!"

"Yes, but most men's mistresses are not Carolyn Travers," Chas pointed out. "Her bloodlines are good, she has a respectable fortune and she's been discreet enough in her affairs to maintain her position in the ton. Not so unlikely, I should think, that she might consider herself a good prospect as a wife. It ain't as though she were some opera dancer."

"There may be something in what you say," Lord Barton admitted. "She did make one or two comments that . . . well, no matter. Captain!"

The captain of the *Cumberland Rover* bowed as he turned to face Barton. "Yes, my lord?" he asked. "What can I do fer yer?"

"I wondered when we would be leaving," Barton asked.

"Jest waiting for the last of my . . . ah! Here they be now," the captain said cheerfully. A group of four or five young men came staggering up the gangplank, singing loudly and trying without success to push one another off the walkway and into the dark water. Lady Augusta Barton, Barton's grandmother, would have branded them a group of fashionable fribbles, with more hair than wit and all pockets to let. As they came on board, one of the young gentlemen stopped and goggled at Lord Barton. "I say," he stammered, "aren't you Barton? I do believe we met in London— at Almack's, perhaps?"

"Indeed," Lord Barton responded dampingly, and turned away. "Our fellow passengers appear a somewhat frivolous lot," he commented to Chas and the captain.

"They ain't so bad, my lord," the captain said. "Me 'Lady Day Lads,' I call 'em." He regarded the passengers happily. "Every year about this time they ship back ter England with me . . . fer quarter day, yer understand. They be headin' back ter see their trustees and get their quarterly allowances."

"After leaving England one step ahead of the bailiffs, one presumes?" Barton said.

"Don't be so self-righteous, Bart," Chas advised him. "Not all of us are as lucky as you."

"I am only a peer, Chas, not a Royal!" Barton reminded his friend. "And you are not so very wealthy, yet I have never seen you obliged to leave the country to avoid your creditors."

"Yes," Chas agreed with a grin, "but I've a rich friend, you see!"

Barton turned back to the captain. "May I take it that we'll be departing forthwith, then?" he asked.

"Indeed we shall, my lord," the captain said. He looked up at the sky. "It'll be a bit dicey crossin' in this weather. I dare say it will add a little ter our time, but have no fear, my lord. We'll make it across all right and tight."

Barton bowed his head to the captain and turned away.

"Well," said Chas, "I'm off to find a large brandy—de la Salle swore to me that it was the only cure for seasickness. Coming, Bart?"

Lord Barton shook his head. "Not I," he replied. "I've still got a head from last night, damn your eyes."

Chas regarded him with amazement. "Why, Bart!" he said reproachfully. "You cannot blame *me* for your own overindulgence, after all!"

Barton grimaced at Chas. "It quite baffles me how you can stand there and talk about being seasick when you have the hardest head of any gentleman I know."

"Spirituous liquors and rolling seas are two completely different things," Chas said loftily. "With spirits one may build up a tolerance, so to speak; I doubt if a thousand sea voyages would ever accustom me to this infernal pitching."

"Well," said Barton, "I wish you and your tolerance well. As for me, I'm off to get a few hours' sleep. A nice quiet cabin is just what I need."

"Sleep?" Chas shuddered. "The very thought of sleeping on this rolling barge of a ship is enough to make me ill. How could you even think of it?"

Barton yawned as he moved away from his friend. "Truth to tell, Chas, at the moment I'm having a difficult time thinking of anything else!" With a wave of his hand, he was gone.

Chas Wendover shuddered. "Sleep!" he muttered, and started off in search of a warm room and a glass of brandy.

LORD BARTON TUGGED his boot off with a grunt and lay back on the bunk. He had not troubled to light the lamp when he entered his cabin; enough dim illumination filtered through the porthole to show him the location of his bed, and he had lost no time in divesting himself of his greatcoat, hat and boots, and making himself comfortable. He lay listening to the sounds of the deck-hands above, readying the ship for sailing. After a few moments, he felt the ship begin to move away from the dock and out into the Channel.

It would be good to be back in London, Barton thought. It had been almost two months since he and his friend Chas had left England to visit France, and though Barton was fond of Paris and the pleasures it had to offer, he was more than ready to return home. He wondered if Carolyn Travers had had time to get over her anger; Lord, but the woman had been in a furious, explosive rage! When Barton had told her that their liaison was at an end, for a moment he had thought that Carolyn would strike him. She had not, of course, but the raven-haired beauty had tried to change Barton's mind with every other trick she knew. She had wept and pleaded, then shouted furiously at him, even going so far as to threaten suicide if Barton did not continue to stand her protector.

The gift of the emeralds had mollified Carolyn somewhat, and she had immediately clasped the necklace about her throat. Barton chuckled to himself as he recalled how adroitly he had made his exit while Carolyn was still busy examining his exquisite gift. All in all, he thought, he had been wise to leave London; by the time he returned to Town, Carolyn should have had more than enough opportunity to recover from losing him. With this hopeful thought, Lord Barton drifted off to sleep.

The night deepened; the *Cumberland Rover* moved farther into the English Channel, and the rolling of the ship became more pronounced. Barton's hat, which he had tossed carelessly onto a chair, slipped off and rolled across the floor of the cabin. Barton's slumber was undisturbed by the motion of the vessel that carried him; he slept on, deep in a dream.

A dark figure slipped out of the shadows of the cabin and moved unsteadily across the pitching floor. When it was almost at the door, a particularly sudden movement of the ship made the figure sink to its knees, with a moan. Several seconds later, the sounds of weak retching disturbed the night-time silence.

Lord Barton awoke with a start. He pushed himself into a sitting position and listened. The faint light that had enabled him to find his bunk earlier was gone; the cabin was pitch-black. The sound that had wakened him was repeated, but louder. "Who's there?" he called. There was no answer. With a muttered oath, Barton swung his legs off the bunk and rose to his feet, groping to find the oil lamp fastened to one wall of the cabin. He stumbled and fell, landing with a thud on something soft. "What the deuce ... ?" Barton sprang to his feet and, having finally located the lamp, lit it.

A girl lay on the floor of his cabin in a crumpled heap. She looked very small, lying there with her eyes closed. Long auburn hair had tumbled down around her shoulders in a tangled mass, and her skin was as white as paper. "What the deuce ... ?" Barton said again.

The girl opened her eyes. "Pray forgive me, sir, but I fear that I am most unwell," she whispered, and turned her face away.

"Devil take it, that's my hat," Barton exclaimed. "You're being ill in my hat!"

The girl lifted her head, exhaustion evident in every line of her body. "I'm sorry," she said. "So very, very sorry!" With that she began to cry quietly.

"Blast it all, don't cry," Barton said sternly. He reached down and scooped the girl up in his arms. He noticed as he did so the neat, though unfashionable, cut of her gown. He also observed that the hands that lay so lightly on his chest had never known manual labour. This girl was no mere bit of muslin, he thought, and deposited her in the bunk. Barton frowned as he looked down at the girl; there was something very familiar about her. She was breathing shallowly through parted lips; and after hesitating for a moment, Barton roughly loosened the laces at her bodice and tucked a blanket around her.

"Please, sir," the girl said frantically. "I fear I shall..." She gulped. "The hat, the hat!"

Barton looked around the cabin wildly for a basin; finding none, with a grimace of distaste he passed his curly-brimmed beaver hat to the girl. When she had finished, he reached into his greatcoat pocket and took out a flask. "Have a little of this," he said, slipping one arm beneath her shoulders. "Yes, yes, I know you don't want it," he added as the girl turned her head away, "but I promise you, it will make you feel very much more the thing." She took a small sip and choked. After a moment or two, Barton lowered her onto the pillow. The girl lay back for several moments before Barton saw a little colour return to her cheeks. "There," he said. "Feeling a bit better?"

"Yes, thank you," the girl said. Brown eyes examined Barton drowsily for a moment, then Barton saw the fear that suddenly struck her. "I must go," she said, clutching at the blanket. "It isn't proper...."

"You need fear nothing from me," Barton said coldly. "Remember, it was not I who sneaked into your cabin."

The girl looked distraught. "Indeed, sir, I did not mean to discommode you," she said. "The cabin was empty when I came in. I thought it a good place to hide. Then, when I heard you coming in, I was so frightened that I hid myself in the cupboard."

"What the...that is to say, why are you hiding? And who are you?" Barton asked, keeping his temper on a tight rein.

"My name is Amanda Stratton," the girl said.

"Stratton?" Barton repeated. "Are you any kin to old General Stratton of Buckinghamshire?"

She nodded shyly. "He was my grandfather," she said. "Did you know him, sir?"

"My grandpapa and he were fast friends," Barton said, his head awhirl. General Stratton had been one of Barton's boyhood heroes; he had know the proud soldier all his life and admired the old gentleman very much. If this girl were his granddaughter, she came from a family of breeding and distinction. Barton searched her face. She did have the look of the general, he was bound to admit. Barton rose to his feet and began to move about the small cabin. "What are you doing here?'' he asked roughly. "Lord above, girl, your grandpapa must be spinning in his grave at the thought of you alone in a gentleman's room. How came you here?''

Amanda Stratton shook her head wearily. "It is too long a story to be told in a trice,'' she said. "And I must leave. As you know, sir, it is most improper for me to be here.''

"A dashed foolish time to be thinking of that,'' Barton said bitterly. "Good God, how do you think you'll ever get out of this cabin without being seen?''

Amanda blinked. "Why, I suppose I shall just wait until the corridor without is empty, and then . . .''

"Exactly,'' said Barton grimly. "And then? This ship is full of gentlemen, and gentlemen of the most unsavoury type, at that. There is no place on board where you could hide with any degree of safety.'' He took another agitated turn about the room, then said, "You will have to stay here. We shall wait until the ship docks and hope that we can spirit you ashore without being seen.''

"But . . .'' Amanda said.

"Have you a better plan?'' Barton asked. "If you do, pray hasten to share it with me.'' Amanda was silent. "All right, then,'' Barton went on. "I shall go up on deck. With the door locked, you should be safe enough here. I'll return and fetch you when we come into the harbour. Mind, now, do not open that door to anyone!''

"Yes, sir,'' Amanda whispered. "And I am truly very, very sorry. . . .''

Barton grunted. He sat down on the edge of the bunk and groped beneath it for his boots. "Damn it all, where are they?" he muttered to himself. "Ah!" He sat back up, boot in hand. Just then the ship rolled, and Lord Barton found himself thrown against the young woman in his bunk. Barton was disconcerted to discover that Amanda's body was softer and more rounded than he would have thought; he struggled to push himself upright.

The door of Barton's cabin opened with a bang, and four young men staggered in, led by the young gentleman whom Barton had snubbed so thoroughly on deck. "Dash it all, I won't wait," the young man said thickly. "He insulted me, and he shall answer for it!"

Chas was bringing up the rear of this motley group. He laid his hand on the aggrieved young man's shoulder. "Come along, now, Forsyth," he was saying, not unkindly. "You're a great deal the worse for wear. Don't cause a quarrel that you will regret."

Barton groaned, and leapt from the bunk. He tried in vain to position himself so that Amanda was invisible to the intruders.

"I say, Barton, I think you owe me an—" The young man stopped, and his eyes widened. "Be damned!" he said.

The other gentleman, too, stopped dead at the sight of Barton and Amanda.

"Well, I like that!" the first young man exclaimed. "He gives me the cut direct, as if he weren't down here frolicking with a prime bit himself."

Chas, after one surprised look, spread his arms wide. "Come along, gentleman," he said. "It's clear we've caught his lordship at a deuced bad time."

One of the other young men broke away from Chas. "Not on your life, Wendover," he said, and hic-coughed. "Perchance his lordship will find it in his heart to introduce this little beauty to us." He sketched a deep, if unsteady, bow. "Good evening, my lady."

Amanda sat frozen, her hands clasped to her cheeks. What little colour her face had fled, then re-turned in a blaze of scarlet.

Barton thought of General Stratton and all that the old man had meant to him. With a sickening feeling of total helplessness he rose to his feet. "You appear to be labouring under a misapprehension, gentlemen," he said coldly. He took Amanda's icy hand in his own. "Allow me to present to you Miss Stratton, who is to be my wife."

Chas Wendover gasped, and Amanda tried desper-ately to pull her hand free, but Barton held it in an iron grip. "You will, of course, perceive the awkwardness of the situation," Barton continued. "Miss Stratton's abigail was inadvertently left behind when the ship sailed. Thus, she is forced to travel without another female to lend her support. When she was taken ill, I was honour bound to see to it that she was properly cared for."

One of the young gentlemen, the one who had begged an introduction, spoke again. "Of all the havey-cavey, witless stories . . . !" he said with a gig-gle.

Chas Wendover spun the young man round to face him. "You would do well," he said quietly, "to keep a civil tongue in your head. Else," Chas added, "I may be compelled to teach you better manners."

The young man gulped. "I—I meant no offence," he stammered. "My apologies." With a sketchy bow, he turned and left the cabin.

"I know that I may rely on all of you to remember that you are gentlemen and keep this unfortunate incident to yourselves," Barton said. "I would be most unhappy to hear rumours of this matter when I return to London." As Barton was well known to be deadly with both sword and pistol, the young men hastily agreed that the matter was forgotten, and left the cabin almost as quickly as their friend had.

Chas lingered for a moment. "Bart!" he said. "What may I do? How can I help?"

Barton smiled bitterly at Chas, a smile that made Chas wince. "Why, you may do the only thing left to be done, old friend," Barton said. "Wish me happy!"

CHAPTER TWO

AMANDA STRATTON slowly opened her eyes. She frowned at the rough wooden ceiling above her and wondered sleepily why Miss Hagstrom had not wakened her. She started to rise, thinking to herself that the little French girl would be bound to be lonely at a new school and in need of comfort, and that she must check on whether or not young Miss Washington had finished her band sampler. Then Amanda sank back on her pillow as she recalled that she was no longer an assistant mistress at Miss Hagstrom's Academy for Young Ladies. Instead, Amanda Stratton found herself stowed away on a ship bound for England. She would never have believed, when she was at Miss Hagstrom's, that she could ever find herself in such a coil. And last night!

Amanda sat up so suddenly that a wave of dizziness washed over her. She looked round the cabin but was relieved to find no sign of the angry gentleman who had proclaimed himself her betrothed. After the small band of gentlemen had left the cabin the night before, Amanda had tried to tell Lord Barton that there was no need for him to pretend to be affianced to her, but he had only looked at her so coldly that Amanda had gasped aloud. "It is a little late for repining now," Barton had said. "The die is cast, Miss Stratton. Your plan has succeeded admirably."

"I don't know what plan you mean," Amanda had responded, bewildered. "I realize that it is not quite the thing for me to have been discovered in your cabin, but I do believe that you are overestimating the importance of the matter."

"Do you?" Barton had said bitterly.

"Those other gentlemen were all . . . well, gentlemen," Amanda had said reasonably. "Surely they may be relied upon to keep silent?"

Barton's expression had grown even colder. "Do not think me a fool, Miss Stratton," he had said. "No one could be so naïve as to think that such a band of scapegraces could be relied upon to hold their tongues—certainly not a young lady with the temerity to hide herself in a gentleman's cabin."

"That was just a coincidence," Amanda pointed out.

"I see." Barton could not have been more coldly and insultingly polite. "It was merely chance that led you to hide in my cabin?"

"Of course it was," Amanda had said impatiently. "Do you think that I intentionally chose it?"

Barton had stunned Amanda by saying, "I think precisely that, as it happens, Miss Stratton." He had gathered his things together and made for the door. As he was leaving the cabin, Barton had turned back and added, "I salute you, madam. Your campaign has been a complete success. You've won the battle." He had smiled coldly. "May you never have cause to regret it!"

Amanda shook her head. She'd had no notion what Barton had been talking about last night, but surely the light of day would have brought him to his senses. And, she hoped, helped him to realize the vanity of his conviction that she had deliberately chosen his cabin to hide in!

Slowly, cautiously, Amanda swung her legs over the side of the bunk. She waited a moment, but after an initial wave of dizziness passed, she found that she felt tolerably well. She surmised that the ship had reached port safely; though the patch of sky visible through the porthole was a threatening grey, the pitching of the ship had settled down to a gentle rocking, and the sounds of purposeful movement from the deck above indicated that passengers were beginning to disembark. Amanda walked across the room to a mirror fixed securely on the wall and shuddered at the sight of herself. Her long auburn hair was matted and greasy with dried sweat; dark shadows surrounded her brown eyes and her skin, Amanda's chief vanity, was pale and grey-hued. Amanda looked round the room. She found a barrel of water in a corner of the cabin and set to cleaning herself with a will.

When a knock came on the cabin door some half hour later, Amanda had done all that was possible, with the limited resources at her disposal, to improve her appearance. She took a deep breath and opened the door.

Amanda saw before her a tall, very thin gentleman with carrot-red hair and a face full of freckles. His expression was rather anxious, but he smiled when he saw Amanda.

"Good morning," he said. "We weren't properly introduced last night, Miss Stratton, but I am Charles Wendover—Chas, for short. I'm a friend of Lord Barton's."

Amanda held out her hand. "I'm very pleased to meet you," she said.

"I must say, you do look a good bit more the thing than you did last night," Chas continued. "Not half so much like a drowned rat!" In truth, Chas was pleasantly surprised by the improvement in Amanda's appearance. Though Amanda's modest gown was not of the best quality and had been sadly crushed overnight, Chas thought that Amanda looked every inch a well-born, gently reared young lady.

Amanda stifled a laugh. "Indeed," she said. "I can only thank God that I no longer *feel* so rat-like!"

He shuddered. "I know just how you feel," he said. "There ain't anything quite as bad as *mal de mer,* is there?" They both laughed.

Chas stopped and cleared his throat, his expression sobering. "The thing is, Bart asked me to come down," he said. "He sends you his compliments and says that he'll be ready to disembark in about twenty minutes."

"Tell his lordship that I thank him for his concern but that I am more than able to see myself off the ship," Amanda said, though her heart sank at the thought of slipping past the captain again, as she had when she came aboard. To the best of her knowledge, the man had no idea that there was a stowaway aboard.

Chas frowned. "I don't think Bart will agree to that," he said. "As a matter of fact, he'll dashed well insist on escorting you ashore, as well he should. It would be scandalous for him to leave his betroth—that is to say, a young lady," he corrected himself hastily, "to see herself home."

"That is most kind in him...." Amanda began impatiently.

"It would be very much better if you just accepted his escort," Chas said firmly.

Amanda wavered for a moment, then gave in. "Very well," she said. "Give his lordship my thanks, and tell him I shall be ready."

"I'll do that," Chas said. He lingered, watching Amanda with a curious expression on his face.

"Is there anything else, Mr. Wendover?" Amanda asked.

Chas started. "No, no, I'll be on my way," he said. He bowed and left her.

Chas was thoughtful when he re-emerged on deck.

"Did you tell her?" Barton asked. Lord Barton was not looking well this morning. After leaving Amanda, he had spent the remainder of the night on deck, drinking brandy. That circumstance, along with the impossibility of changing his clothes—they were in his cabin—had left Barton looking unkempt enough to astonish Chas.

"Good God, Bart, at least splash some water on your head before she comes up," Chas said. "You look like a deuced criminal."

"My betrothed will have to take me as she finds me," Barton growled.

Chas frowned. "Bart," he said hesitantly, "are you quite sure that Miss Stratton is a...well, that she trapped you?"

Barton snorted, then grimaced. "Damn, but I've the headache!" he groaned. "As to your question, yes, Chas, I am quite sure," he continued. "If you could have heard her last night, protesting that it was sheer coincidence that she chose my cabin to hide in. She must think me a fool!"

"It could have been an accident," Chas pointed out.

"You forget that Miss Stratton is not the first lady to set her sights on me," Barton said. "Believe me, Chas, when you've eluded as many traps as I have, you learn to recognize one when you see it."

"But she seems so unexceptionable," Chas said, frowning. "I should have thought her an ordinary young lady of gentle birth, by her appearance."

"Ah, but she plays her part too well," Barton retorted. "She told me that I was making too much of the matter, and that surely we could rely on the discretion of the other gentlemen involved."

"Well?"

"Chas, that young woman cannot be much younger than twenty or twenty-one," Barton said. "Do you really mean to tell me that any girl of her background could reach that age without having been warned of the dangers of being alone with a gentleman?"

"Perhaps not," Chas agreed reluctantly.

"Definitely not," Barton said. "If she knew enough of Society to choose the cabin of the only well-heeled gentleman aboard in the first place, then she knew enough to know exactly what position she was placing me in." He grinned sourly. "And so the mighty Lord Barton is brought down!"

Chas was silent for a long moment. Then he said carefully, "Well, if you're so sure that she entrapped you, perhaps you shouldn't marry her, after all. You needn't look at me that way," he added hastily as his friend stared at him. "I know that in the normal way of things, you'd never consider avoiding your duty, but, damn it all, Bart! This ain't exactly the ordinary way of things."

"True enough," Barton allowed. He rubbed a hand over his whiskered face. "But how can I not wed the chit, Chas? General Stratton was her grandpapa—General Stratton, the man who was my own grandfather's best friend, and someone I admired enormously myself. Everything else aside, I could never show such disrespect to the general's memory."

"Maybe she's not really a Stratton at all," Chas suggested.

Barton shook his head. "Not a chance of it," he said gloomily. "Her resemblance to the general is striking. Given enough time, I think I would have known her as a Stratton if she'd never told me her name." Barton sighed, then threw his shoulders back and flashed a rueful smile at Chas. "No, Chas my boy, she has me," he said. "Whether I will it or not—and I most certainly do not!—Miss Stratton and I shall wed, as soon as we return to London."

"I wish there were some way I might help," Chas said.

"There is," Barton answered. "Come round and see me tomorrow—there will be a thousand details to attend to if the marriage is to take place immediately, and I won't have time to see to everything and keep an eye on our Miss Stratton, too.''

"Of course," Chas said.

"And find your own way back to Town, won't you? My betrothed and I shall travel in my carriage." Barton smiled grimly as the skies opened and rain began to fall. "Miss Amanda Stratton and I have a great deal to talk about!"

AMANDA SANK BACK against the squabs of the carriage with a sigh of relief. Over the steady drumming of the rain on the roof she could hear the murmur of Barton's voice as he spoke to the coachman. She pushed back her dripping hood and slipped the sodden cloak from her shoulders as the carriage door opened again and Barton entered, seating himself opposite her as the vehicle began to move.

"I must thank you, my lord," Amanda said, "for being so kind as to escort me off the ship. I did not relish the thought of facing the captain."

Barton did not answer her. He stared out the carriage window, his expression grim.

"He looked so very angry," Amanda continued nervously. "The captain, that is to say. How he did glare as we left the ship!"

"He has no reason to be angry any longer," Barton said. "Your passage has been paid."

Amanda sat up straight. "You should not have done that, my lord," she said. "Was it very dear? I'm afraid . . . I'm afraid I may not have the means to repay you."

Barton looked at her, and Amanda winced. "Let us have done with this charade, shall we?" Barton said coldly. "Is there anyone who should be notified as to your whereabouts?"

"No!" Amanda cried. "That is to say... no, thank you, my lord. If you would just let me off at an inexpensive inn, I should be most grateful. And of course I shall do my very best to repay you for my passage as soon as I can."

"You shall stay at my house in Grosvenor Square until I can make the proper arrangements," Barton said. He looked Amanda over, then added, "And we shall have to see about getting you some clothes."

"You'll do no such thing," Amanda said, clasping her hands tightly to keep them from trembling. "I know that you may have got somewhat the wrong notion about... well, about the sort of person I am..."

Barton snorted. "I know exactly what sort of person you are," he said. "But I'm damned if the rest of the ton will! From now on, until we are married and after, you will conduct yourself with perfect propriety."

"Married?" Amanda said. "Are you run mad?" She stopped and took a deep breath. "Perhaps I did not make myself quite clear on the subject, my lord," she said. "I have no desire, no, nor intention of marrying you. Why, I don't even know you!"

"You should have thought of that before you trapped me," Barton growled.

"For the last time, I did not trap you!" Amanda said. "I've told you over and over I chose your cabin by accident, an accident which I deeply regret."

"I see," said Barton. "It was by mere coincidence that you chose to linger in the cabin of the only gentleman on board who was not pockets to let. Now why do I find that so difficult to believe?"

"Because you are insufferably puffed up with your own conceit!" Amanda snapped. "A more prideful creature I have never met."

"That may well be," Barton said. "But, since it is that selfsame pride which compels me to marry you, you shouldn't complain of it."

"I will not marry you!" Amanda all but shouted, her face flushed. "Let me out of this carriage immediately. I shall find my own way to London."

"Pray do not be so tiresome," Barton said. "Your plan has succeeded admirably—will you lose your courage now, when the prize is in your hand?"

"I can only presume that your hearing is defective, my lord," Amanda retorted. "As I have told you, there is no plan." She laughed bitterly. "I simply chose the wrong ship!"

Barton leaned back against the cushions of the carriage. His head hurt, and he was very tired.

Amanda fought to control her temper and leaned forward in her seat. "I do understand that the circumstances are unusual," she said earnestly. "Let me tell you how I came to be aboard the *Cumberland Rover*."

"Thank you, but no. The subject holds no interest for me, I assure you."

"But you don't understand . . . !"

"I understand perfectly," Barton said curtly. "You set out to trap yourself a rich husband, and you've done the job quickly and efficiently. There is no need, at this late date, to spin me some taradiddle about your unhappy life. You've won, my dear, you've won! Now pray leave me in silence until we reach London."

"Why must you be so hateful?" Amanda demanded. "Though I have no intention of marrying you, I should still like to explain. . . ."

Barton pressed a hand to his aching head. "Since you apparently will not leave me in peace until I play out this scene, so be it," he said, sitting up. "If we do not wed, you will be ruined, as well you know, and I will be reviled as a cad and a seducer."

"You overstate the matter, my lord," Amanda said. "I shall not be ruined, for I do not move in the circles where such things matter. In point of fact, I am going to London to seek employment as a governess. As for your reputation—well, I am sorry. But I dare say the talk will die down quickly, and you may go on comfortably with your life."

"Will you give up this pretence of stupidity, madam?" Barton said. "Any family in a position to hire a governess would also be in a position to hear the gossip—there is no chance that you would be able to find a position. If you did, you would last exactly as long as it took your employers to hear the whispers. Then you would be turned out at once."

"Surely it would not make such a great scandal as that?" Amanda said uncertainly.

"It would," Barton told her. "I am fairly well-known to London Society, and those bounders who burst in on us would not lose a minute in spreading the story all over Town."

"Then what difference does it make whether or not we wed?" Amanda retorted. "If you are so sure they'll spread the story..."

"Not if we are married," Barton said grimly. "I doubt if any of those young bucks would have the courage to speak against my wife."

"The country," Amanda said, a note of desperation in her voice. "I could go to the country and seek a position. Surely the gossip would not travel so far?"

"It would, in time," Barton said, "as I'm sure you knew when you planned your... campaign, shall we call it?"

Amanda shook her head. "How can I convince you that there was no *campaign?*" she said. "Why won't you listen?"

"Because," Barton snapped, "I have heard quite enough!" He let down the window, stuck out his head and roared, "Spring 'em, man! I want to reach London today, not next week."

The coachman, too well trained to argue with his master, shook out the reins and the carriage shot forward through the driving rain. Amanda was unpleasantly reminded of the heaving decks of the *Cumberland Rover;* she closed her eyes and pressed one hand to her stomach as the body of the carriage swayed back and forth. Just when she thought that she could not tolerate the motion for another moment, the vehicle gave a great lurch and she was thrown from her seat.

Amanda landed squarely in Lord Barton's lap. His arms closed around her as the carriage shuddered, then began to slide sideways.

"What the devil . . . ?" Barton exclaimed. He tightened his hold on Amanda as the vehicle tipped and they were both thrown from the seat into a corner of the carriage.

For a moment, they lay still. Amanda had landed on top of Barton, still held fast in his arms. Despite her upset, she found herself very much aware of his body, pressed so tightly against her. She had never been so close to a gentleman before; his warm strength surprised her, as did his faint, pleasantly masculine smell.

"We must have gone into a ditch," Barton said. "Are you hurt?"

"I don't think so," she said breathlessly. Barton's face was only inches from her own; his eyes were very blue, she saw, and curiously deep, like cool, clear water. For one long moment, she found herself unable to look away. "And . . . and you?"

"Unscathed," Barton said gruffly. "Fortunately, you are not weighty enough to have done me any serious damage!" Indeed, he was amazed, and not a little disconcerted, by the feel of Amanda's body against his own. The rain had moulded her clothing to her, and Barton was acutely conscious of her every curve.

The door that was now over their heads was pulled open and the coachman's head appeared. "My lord— are ye hurt?" he asked anxiously.

Amanda blushed hotly and struggled to push herself away from Barton. "What the devil happened?" Barton asked irritably.

"It were a powerful big stone, right smack in the middle o' the road. How it came there I've nary a notion, but I never even saw it for the rain."

"Is the carriage very badly damaged?"

The coachman grinned. "You'll never credit it, my lord, but it looks to be fine! On account o' the mud, ye see, it just sort o' slid, like."

"Excellent," Barton said. "Then if you'll be so good as to give me a hand, we can be on our way. The sooner this nightmare journey is ended, the better!"

AMANDA STRATTON and Lord Barton arrived in London late that evening. Amanda was exhausted; a night of seasickness, followed by a hard day's travel and a jarring accident, had left her feeling drained and shaky. And the long journey, which Barton had insisted must be completed that day, had also given Amanda too much time to brood on her current situation. All the way from Bristol she had chased round and round the problem of her betrothal to Barton; unfortunately, the more Amanda thought about it, the more she was bound to admit that Barton was probably right. Barton's obvious disinclination to wed her lent credence to his reasons why they must marry. Clearly he would not exaggerate those reasons, but must truly believe that Amanda, and to a lesser extent Barton himself, would be ruined if they did not wed. Amanda was stunned at the thought of spending the rest of her life with this surly, ill-kempt man who made it quite clear that he despised her. It was all Amanda could do to stifle a bitter laugh. She had jumped, it would seem, straight from the frying pan into the fire!

As the carriage pulled up before Barton's house in Grosvenor Square, Amanda promised herself that she would think of some way out of this coil as soon as she had had a good night's sleep.

Barton jumped down from the carriage. He waved the footman away and helped Amanda down himself, tucking her arm firmly into his own. "Just be silent and let me explain your presence," he muttered to Amanda as they approached the front door. "There's no need to give the servants any more to gossip about than we must." The front door opened.

"Good evening, Dennison," Barton said pleasantly as the butler bowed them into the house.

The butler bent his head gravely. He was a short, squat man who looked as though he would benefit from a day in the sunshine. "Good evening, my lord," he said. "If I may say so, it is good to have you home."

Amanda looked curiously around the entrance hall. The black-and-white tiled floor was glossy with wax, and double staircases swept upwards in graceful curves to meet halfway up the high-ceilinged space, where a large portrait of a formidable-looking old gentleman hung. The walls of the hall were hung with pale yellow silk; a huge mahogany table stood in the middle of the floor with a silver bowl of fresh spring flowers precisely in its centre.

"Dennison," Barton said, "allow me to present to you Miss Amanda Stratton. I know that you will wish me happy when I tell you that Miss Stratton has graciously agreed to be my wife."

Dennison blinked, hesitating for a moment before inclining his head. "My congratulations, my lord, Miss Stratton," he said stiffly. "This is wonderful news indeed." Dennison's manner was not lost on Amanda, who felt the colour flood into her cheeks at the butler's disapproval.

"There's been a most unfortunate accident, though," Barton continued blandly. "Miss Stratton's baggage was inadvertently left in France when our ship sailed. Would you see if Mrs. Mandley can find her something to sleep in until she may acquire new clothing?"

The butler looked sceptically at Amanda. She burned with embarrassment as he answered, "As you wish, my lord."

"Very good," Barton said. Taking hold of Amanda's arm again, he steered her into the library that opened off the entrance hall.

"Of all the weak-witted stories I've ever heard, that was the worst," Amanda said as Barton shut the door behind them. "Did you see the way he looked at me?"

"Did you expect me to tell him that your bags fell overboard?" Barton snapped. "If you did not wish to be looked at askance, you should never have placed yourself in such shocking circumstances."

"You are the most insufferable..." Amanda began.

"Yes, yes, you've told me all that before," Barton said impatiently. "Sit down." He indicated a chair. Amanda only glared at him, so he repeated loudly, "Sit down!"

After a moment's hesitation, Amanda obeyed him. The library was every bit as luxuriously appointed as the foyer. A fire burned in the hearth, making the polished brass fenders shine and reflecting off the crystal decanters that stood on a sideboard. A thick Persian rug lay on the floor and the chairs were leather, deep and wonderfully comfortable. Amanda shrank back into the depths of her seat despondently, for it was beginning to dawn on her that perhaps Barton had not been merely prideful in considering himself such a desirable parti.

Barton regarded his fiancée with a frown. "Here," he said abruptly, crossing the room. "Have a sherry. You're looking a trifle pale."

"No, thank you, my lord," Amanda said. "I do not drink spirits."

"That may be," Barton said, returning to Amanda's side with a full glass, "but I'm damned if the servants will see me carrying you out of this room in a swoon. Drink it."

Amanda took a sip and wrinkled her nose. After a moment, she took another sip, and then another. "It is very... very warming, is it not?" she said.

"Indeed," Barton agreed drily. He poured himself a brandy and sat down behind the large desk that dominated the library. "Now," he said. "I shall be going to an hotel tonight. It would not be proper for both of us to stay here without another lady to chaperon us."

"Surely it is I who should leave?" Amanda said. "After all, this is your home."

"Yes, that would make a pretty picture, wouldn't it?" Barton said. "A young lady turning up at an hotel with no baggage and no abigail to lend her countenance. They'd have you out in the street before you had time to tell them your name. No, you've done quite enough damage to both our reputations for one day. You'll stay here."

"Very well, my lord," Amanda said tiredly.

"First thing in the morning, I'll be off to obtain a special licence," Barton went on. "There should be no difficulty. Plan on the wedding taking place tomorrow afternoon."

"I won't...I can't...." Amanda fell silent. All of a sudden, she had not the strength to argue with Barton any longer.

"In the meantime, I'll have Mrs. Mandley take you out tomorrow to get some new clothes. Purchase whatever you'll need and have the bills sent to me." Barton dashed back the rest of his brandy and pulled the cord for Dennison. "Dennison will show you to your rooms. I'll have him send up a kitchen maid to see to your needs until you can hire an abigail." Lord Barton took up his hat and cane and bowed deeply before Amanda. "Until tomorrow, my sweet," he said with a sardonic smile, and was gone.

CHAPTER THREE

THE NEXT MORNING, Chas Wendover appeared just after breakfast to take Amanda driving. Amanda was feeling very much more the thing; a good night's sleep in a comfortable bed, and the unaccustomed pleasure of having a maid to wait on her had worked wonders on her frame of mind. Her brown twill redingote had been brushed clean and pressed overnight, and a hot bath had restored her long auburn hair to its customary sheen and neatness. While Amanda knew that she could not pretend to be fashionable, at the very least she looked tidy and presentable.

Chas seemed to agree with her. "You appear to be much restored, Miss Stratton," he said cheerfully as he escorted Amanda to his phaeton. "I dare say the opportunity to bathe and sleep in a stationary bed did not come amiss?"

"It was wonderful," Amanda confessed. "I have never spent such a comfortable night. Meg, the maid that my lord Barton sent up to help me, was very kind. And Mrs. Mandley says that we are to go shopping this afternoon! I must allow, I have never been so pampered before."

Chas looked at Amanda, surprised by her naïve enthusiasm. "I'm sure Bart will be glad to hear that his people have seen to your needs so well," he said. "Truth to tell, his staff have an inordinately easy time of it—Bart is very often away from home, and when he is in London, he rarely entertains or has house guests." Chas adroitly feathered a corner with his phaeton and pulled into Hyde Park.

"How very beautiful it is!" Amanda said, looking about the Park. "I must confess, I had begun to think that there were no open spaces left in all of London."

"Have you never been to Town before, Miss Stratton?" Chas asked.

"No, indeed—or rather, not since I was too young to remember it," Amanda said. "I have always wished to, though! I used to dream about what it would be like to live in Town, to go to balls and routs, and shopping whenever one had a mind to, to visit the opera and the theatre.... It always sounded to me as though London must be the most exciting place in the world." Her face fell. "I never thought my first visit would come about in such a way," she finished in a tone so woebegone that Chas felt a stir of pity for her.

"Well, I dare say you'll find it every bit as exciting as you had dreamed," he said. "You'll be run off your feet once you and Bart are married. There won't be an entertainment or evening of any size that you won't be invited to."

Amanda looked down at her hands, folded tightly in her lap. "How can I marry Lord Barton?" she asked. "It is madness even to think of it."

Chas shook his head and shot a warning look towards his groom, perched on the back of the phaeton. He pulled the vehicle over to the side of the roadway and said, "Rivers, hold the horses, if you please. I'm going to take Miss Stratton down to walk along the Serpentine—we shall be back in a few moments." The servant obeyed, and Barton's friend helped Amanda down. When they were out of earshot of the groom, Chas asked sternly, "Now, what is this nonsense about not marrying Barton? Don't you realize that you'll be ruined if you don't?"

Amanda pressed a hand to her eyes. "How did I ever find myself in this coil?" she asked herself aloud. "How?"

"Well, that's a question I should like an answer to myself," Chas said frankly. "Mean to say, Miss Stratton, you certainly don't seem like an..." He stopped.

"An adventuress?" supplied Amanda bleakly.

"Exactly," Chas said with a grin. "Not meaning to be disloyal to Bart, but you've made quite a favorable impression on me, taken all in all. I wish you would tell me how you came to be aboard that cursed ship." He watched Amanda's face, then added gently, "You stand in need of a friend, my dear. Won't you let me be one?"

Amanda was obliged to blink back tears. Chas's words were the first kindness she had been offered since she left Miss Hagstrom's, and the sympathetic smile that Chas turned on her made her defences crumble. "It's rather a long story...." she began.

"I was orphaned at a very early age, when both my parents were killed in a coach accident," Amanda said. "My father's father, General Stratton, was far too old to take charge of a young child, and my mother had no living family, so I was sent to Miss Hagstrom's Academy for Young Ladies. I was very happy there. Miss Hagstrom is a kind-hearted woman, and she made me feel as though she truly cared about my welfare. When I was seven, my grandfather, who had been paying all my school bills, died. He left a small legacy, enough to finish paying for my education, and appointed my uncle, Cecil Stratton, as my guardian. I continued at the school until I was seventeen, when, in the normal course of things, it would have been time for me to make my debut.''

Amanda dropped her eyes and began to fiddle with the strings of her reticule. ''But my uncle Cecil wrote to Miss Hagstrom to say that he was unable to have me with him at that time, and that he was also unable to continue to pay my keep. He suggested that Miss Hagstrom keep me on as an assistant. Miss Hagstrom agreed, and so I remained at the academy.''

''That don't seem at all the thing,'' Chas said doubtfully. ''A girl of your birth shouldn't be working as a schoolmarm's assistant.''

''In truth, I was not unhappy,'' Amanda said. ''Miss Hagstrom's was the only home that I had ever known. Oh, I will admit to a little disappointment at not being able to come out, but, all things considered, my life was a contented one. I stayed there for another three years.'' Amanda fell silent.

''And then?'' Chas prompted her.

''And then, about two weeks ago, my uncle Cecil suddenly appeared out of nowhere to take me out of school,'' Amanda said. ''I was stunned, for I did not know him, but I was also pleased—I thought that at last I should have the debut I had always dreamed of. It was not to be, however—Uncle Cecil and I left immediately for France. Once we arrived there, I learned that my uncle had a plan for me." Amanda did not look at Chas. "He took me to an old château in the south of France. Once there, he told me that without my knowledge or permission, he had betrothed me to the Vicomte DeValme."

Chas drew in his breath. *"L'Ange infame?"* he said. "But...he's a rotter! His reputation..." Chas's words trailed to a halt. The Vicomte DeValme was famous, or infamous, far beyond the borders of his native France. Known as *l'Ange infame,* for his beautiful face, corrupt manner and the habit he had of always wearing black, DeValme was a despoiler of women and a devotee of the more notorious pleasures of life.

"Indeed," Amanda agreed drily. "I know that I am unlearned in the ways of the world, but even I had heard of DeValme and his depravity. I told my uncle that I would not marry DeValme, not for any consideration."

"Bravo!" Chas said.

"Uncle Cecil told me that my consent was not necessary to the match. He said that he, as my guardian, had the right to choose a husband for me. He told me that I would not leave the château until the wedding was performed. He was...he was most unkind." Amanda's eyes darkened at the memory.

"It's like something from a novel," Chas said. "What did you do?"

"One night when Cecil was away from home, I managed to sneak out of the château under the cover of darkness," Amanda said. "I made my way to Calais—quite fortunately I had learned to speak fluent French at Miss Hagstrom's—and stowed away on the first ship leaving for England, which was the *Cumberland Rover*." Amanda looked at Chas anxiously. "I knew no one in France, you see, except for Uncle Cecil and...DeValme. Where was I to turn? I felt I had no choice."

"My dear girl, of course you didn't," Chas said. "What a story! You have been misused quite dreadfully."

"Now perhaps you can understand why I will not marry Lord Barton," Amanda said earnestly. "He despises me! I did not run away from one unwanted marriage only to enter into another."

"It is wrong of you to compare Bart with that fiend DeValme," Chas told Amanda. "Bart is a good man. Once you've told him your story, he'll see how this all came about."

Amanda shook her head. "I tried," she said. "I begged him to listen! But he told me not to trouble him with my 'taradiddles.' He hates me. He would never believe anything I said."

"I'll tell him, then," Chas said. "You needn't worry. Bart will understand, just as I have."

"Thank you, but no," she said, smiling wanly. "Yours is the first friendly face I've seen since I left Miss Hagstrom's. I couldn't bear it if you were to suffer because you have befriended me."

"That wouldn't happen," Chas began. "Bart and I—"

"You don't know how he dislikes me," Amanda interrupted him. "He would be angry with you for defending me, and to what purpose? He would still not believe me."

"But..."

"No!" Amanda said. "You said that you would be my friend, Mr. Wendover. If you are truly my friend, promise me that you will not tell Lord Barton."

"Very well," Chas agreed grudgingly. "But you are being exceptionally foolish, you know. Your marriage to Barton would be a much happier one if only you'd tell him the truth."

"I do not intend to marry Lord Barton," Amanda said obstinately. She clutched Chas's arm. "You can help me—escort me back to Miss Hagstrom's! I know she'd take me in. I could simply resume my duties there. It would be as though I'd never left."

"It wouldn't work," Chas said gently. "Miss Hagstrom caters to daughters of the ton, does she not?" Amanda nodded. "Then she would be able to keep you at the academy for precisely as long as it took the gossip to reach there, at which point she would be obliged to let you go."

"Miss Hagstrom cares about me," Amanda protested. "She would never turn me away."

"Then she'd lose all her pupils," Chas said bluntly. "No one would leave their daughter in a school that employed a woman of questionable reputation."

"How do you know that she would ever hear the gossip?" Amanda said. "Surely you're overestimating the ill will of the other passengers on the ship? They'll have forgotten the whole matter before long,

I have no doubt." She smiled sourly. "I doubt that my Lord Barton is quite so enthralling a topic of conversation as he believes himself to be."

"You could not be more wrong," Chas said. "Barton's family is one of the oldest and proudest in England. Barton himself is a leader of Society, much admired for his honour and integrity. Were a rumour to surface that he had behaved scandalously, Barton's name would be bruited about the length and breadth of England."

Amanda fought back gamely. "I'm sure that a few ill-natured people might whisper, but surely the talk would not be so widespread as all that? After all, if he is so much admired..."

Chas grimaced. "Gossip is the meat and drink of the ton," he said. "Because Barton has been such a leader of Society, those less favoured would delight in dragging him down. They'd keep the story going for weeks, perhaps even months."

Amanda looked at Chas so unhappily that Chas's heart went out to her. "But how can I marry him?" she asked miserably. "How can I marry a complete stranger, and one who despises me?"

"Don't confuse Bart with DeValme," Chas said. "Bart may not have looked to be married, but this I do know—he is a decent and principled man. He'll be as good a husband to you as he is able."

Amanda laughed bitterly. "How good a husband can he be when he loathes the very thought of marriage?"

"There is another factor you may not have considered," Chas said. "Has it occurred to you that if you do not wed Barton, your uncle may very well come and take you back to France to marry DeValme?''

Amanda drew in her breath. "He couldn't—could he?''

"There is nothing to stop him, short of your marriage to someone else,'' Chas pointed out. "Cecil is your guardian. Legally, he has every right to choose a mate for you.'' Chas glanced at Amanda out of the corner of his eye; he saw by her stricken expression that the notion had not occurred to her. After they had walked along in silence for a few moments, Chas went on, "Will you promise me something, Amanda—may I call you Amanda?''

"You might just as well,'' Amanda said with the ghost of a smile. "You are my only friend in London, after all.''

"I want you to promise me that you'll give up this idea of running away. Believe me, my dear, it will not answer,'' Chas said soberly. "As reluctant as you may be to wed Barton, the alternatives are far, far worse. Will you promise?''

"Yes,'' Amanda said. "Whatever I do, I shan't run away. You've quite convinced me that I've nowhere to go!''

"You've made a wise decision, my dear,'' Chas said. He led her back to the phaeton and handed her up into her seat. He leaned forward as he settled himself behind the reins and murmured, too quietly for the groom to hear, "Never look so tragic, my dear—you may find that this marriage is not half so bad as you anticipate!''

WILLIAM, LORD BARTON stood at one end of the drawing-room, beside the clergyman who would marry him to Amanda Stratton. He looked with sardonic amusement at the flowers that filled the room; Mrs. Mandley, the housekeeper, had insisted on decorating the room suitably once she learned that a wedding was to take place. Barton had realized that if he did not make some show of wanting to be wed, it would cause even more talk among the servants, so he had acquiesced to the housekeeper's scheme with as much aplomb as he could manage.

Doctor Lincoln, the clergyman, cleared his throat nervously. "My lord," he said, then stopped. "My lord, I hope you will not mind...that is to say, I intend no offense...."

Barton looked at him quizzically. "Yes?"

The little clergyman drew himself up. "My lord, due to the...ah, unusual circumstances, I should like to have a quiet word with the bride before the ceremony begins. If you have no objections, that is?" Doctor Lincoln fixed Barton with an anxious stare.

"None whatsoever," Barton said smoothly. The parson looked greatly relieved and turned his attention back to his prayer-book. Barton stifled his irritation. Damn it all, one couldn't blame the man for being suspicious, given the indecent speed with which the marriage had been arranged!

The double doors at the end of the room opened, and Amanda Stratton came in on Chas's arm. One of Barton's eyebrows soared upward; he was bound to admit that Amanda looked very well indeed. She had chosen a simple gown of dull golden silk; her hair tumbled down her back, held in place by a thin gold fillet and in her arms she carried a bouquet of white roses.

Amanda halted involuntarily at the sight of Barton. Could this handsome and elegant gentleman be the same unkempt, surly man who had escorted her from Bristol? Barton was attired in a blue superfine frock-coat that fit him like a glove; his intricately arranged neckcloth was secured by one large sapphire that exactly matched the colour of his eyes. Unshaven, unwashed and in day-old clothing, Barton had not been much to look at, but now Amanda saw that it was not only Barton's fortune that made him so attractive to the ladies of the ton.

Chas, misinterpreting the reason for Amanda's hesitation, patted her hand. "Courage, little one," he said with a reassuring smile. "It will all be over soon."

Amanda took a deep breath and resumed her slow progress towards the end of the room. She passed Barton's servants, who had been invited to attend the wedding. They stared at her curiously and, as soon as she had passed them, began to whisper among themselves. Amanda ignored them. She found it difficult to remove her gaze from Barton, yet when he met her eyes, she looked away and blushed furiously.

When Chas and Amanda reached Barton, the peer bowed to Amanda. "Doctor Lincoln," he said distantly, "would like to have a word with you before the ceremony begins."

Chas looked curiously at his friend as Amanda and the clergyman moved away. "What's that all about?" he asked, jerking his head towards the pair.

"The good parson," growled Barton, "wishes to be sure that I am not coercing Miss Stratton into marriage. A good joke, that, eh?"

Chas frowned. "Bart," he said slowly, "I think you're making a mistake."

Barton smiled sourly. "I don't doubt it, but sadly, it is too late to repine."

"That's not what I meant," Chas said. "I was speaking of Amanda. She's not what you think her, Bart."

"Has she won you over so easily, then?" Barton asked. "It appears that my bride-to-be is a woman of formidable charms."

"Not at all," Chas said. "Well, she is charming, I suppose, but . . . dash it all, Bart, the child has not the least notion of how to go on!"

"She's managed to get what she wanted from me easily enough," Barton said. He held up a hand when Chas opened his mouth to continue. "No, Chas, that's enough," he said. "I will marry Miss Stratton, but I'm damned if she'll make me like it!"

A short distance away, Doctor Lincoln was peering at Amanda anxiously. "Are you quite sure, my dear, that you are entering into this marriage of your own free will?"

Amanda closed her eyes for a moment and thought of all that had happened to her since Uncle Cecil had removed her from Miss Hagstrom's. The trip to France, her flight from marriage to the Vicomte

DeValme, that awful night on the *Cumberland Rover*—all had led her inevitably to this moment. Amanda recalled Chas's warning about what would become of her if she did not marry Lord Barton. She shuddered at the thought of being forced to marry DeValme after all she had gone through to escape him. Amanda opened her eyes and, with a sick feeling of finality, said, "Yes, sir. It is my wish to be wed."

Lord Barton and Amanda Stratton were joined in marriage with a minimum of fuss. The ceremony took no more than a few moments; Chas Wendover and Barton's housekeeper, Mrs. Mandley, served as witnesses to the match. As soon as the ceremony was completed, Barton's servants clustered around the newlyweds to offer their felicitations to Barton and their new mistress.

Barton accepted their congratulations patiently. He shook hands and smiled at his dependants, even going so far as to accept Mrs. Mandley's roguish kiss. Then he took Amanda firmly by the arm. "I know that you will forgive me," he said, speaking both to his servants and to Chas, "if I wish to be private with my bride. Good night to you all, and I thank you for your good wishes."

"Bart..." Chas began worriedly.

"Good night, Chas," Barton said with finality. With that, he steered Amanda out of the drawing-room.

As soon as the door closed behind them, her husband released Amanda's arm. "Go upstairs," he said flatly. "I've several matters to attend to before I retire—I'll join you shortly."

Amanda gasped. "I beg your pardon?"

One corner of Barton's mouth lifted in a sardonic smile. "Need I remind you that we were just wed? It would be thought passing strange, did we not spend our wedding night together. Don't you agree?"

"But...I..." Amanda looked up at him, blushing furiously.

"Exactly," Barton said. He bowed his head mockingly. "And if it's any consolation to you, my dear, I like the notion no more than you do!"

AMANDA SAT before the dressing-table in her room while Meg, the maid, brushed her long auburn hair.

"What lovely hair you have, my lady," the maid volunteered shyly. "It's just like silk, it is."

"Thank you, Meg," Amanda said, striving to maintain a light tone. "I must allow, I've often thought of cutting it—the latest fad is for short, curly hair, is it not? And long hair is a great deal of trouble."

"Ah, but you'll never convince me that the gentlemen don't prefer it long," Meg said with all the wisdom of her eighteen years. "They like a lady to look a lady and not a boy, is what I always say!" She tied Amanda's hair loosely at the nape of her neck with a pink ribbon, and stepped back. "There," she said, satisfied. "You do look a picture, my lady."

Amanda smiled wanly. "Thank you, Meg," she said. "You've been very kind."

"Now, is there anything else you'll be needing before I go?" the servant asked solicitously. Amanda shook her head. Impulsively, Meg reached out and squeezed her mistress's hand. "No need to look so nervous, ma'am," she said with a reassuring smile. "It's lucky you are, you know, to be wed to such a one as Lord Barton. There's many a lady as will be crushed to hear he's taken!" She bobbed a curtsy and left the room.

Amanda pushed herself away from the dressing-table and began to drift aimlessly about the room, the fine cotton of her nightdress swirling about her ankles. Meg was right, she thought. The handsome, well-dressed gentleman who had exchanged wedding vows with her must have set many a heart aflutter in his bachelor days. How many ladies, she wondered, would have given anything to be in her place tonight? She was forced to admit to herself that this was a man who might, under different circumstances, have been everything that she could ever have hoped for in a husband.

Amanda moved to the fireplace and stared blindly down into the flames. How she wished that her marriage had come about in the traditional way! What would it have been like to have known herself to have been chosen for love? What would it have been like to be the object of Barton's desire? In her mind's eye she saw again the lean, chiselled profile of her husband; she recalled the feel of his hard body against hers in the carriage and shivered. Lost in her musings, Amanda did not hear the bedchamber door open.

Barton paused on the threshold. As he watched Amanda look into the dying fire, he realized, with something of a shock, that his bride was very beautiful. In the dim, flickering light her hair was like a russet cloud and her skin glowed; the thin lawn of her nightdress did little to conceal her charms, but rather, enhanced them. For a fleeting moment, he wondered what it would be like to hold this girl in his arms, to kiss her and caress her smooth skin. Then Amanda sighed, and the spell was broken. Barton came into the room and shut the door firmly behind him.

Amanda jumped. "Oh!" she said. "I—I didn't hear you, my lord." She observed his brocade dressing-gown with alarm, looked down at her own nightdress and blushed hotly. Barton watched with grim amusement as she sidled towards the bed, got in and pulled the sheets up to her chin.

"I shall be leaving first thing in the morning," he said without preamble, "and there are several matters we should discuss before I go."

Amanda stared at him stupidly. "What?" she said. "Where are you going?"

"To Herefordshire, to break the news of my marriage to my grandmother," he said. "Needless to say, I should prefer that she did not learn of it through reading the newspapers." Barton placed a sheet of foolscap beside the candles on Amanda's dressing-table. "This is the name of my man of business. I've arranged for an allowance to be settled on you, and I've left fifty pounds in the library for you. If you need any further funds, simply advise Mr. Ransom and he will set up a drawing account."

"I thank you, my lord, but I have no need of your money," Amanda said proudly.

"Yes, I'm sure," Barton said in a withering tone. "You will prove to be the most frugal of wives, I have no doubt."

"Why must you be so hateful?" Amanda asked. She met Barton's gaze squarely. "Now that we are wed, mightn't we try to be...well, at least civil to each other?"

"The marriage changed nothing," Barton said flatly. "If you thought that once the deed was done you might beguile me into acceptance of it, then you were sadly mistaken, my dear." He blew out the candles and she heard him remove his dressing-gown. He slid into the bed, but made no attempt to move closer to Amanda. "In short," he added, "though you may be my wife in name, that is all that you shall ever be!"

CHAPTER FOUR

LADY AUGUSTA BARTON paused on the threshold of the drawing-room, her thin hand clenched around the knob of an ebony walking-stick. Her slender frame, perfectly erect despite her seventy years, was clad in crisp black silk. A plain white cap covered her sedately coiffed silver hair; she wore no jewellery but the gold wedding band on her left hand.

Lady Augusta was a proud but loving woman, the daughter of an earl, who had lived her whole life without the breath of scandal ever touching her. She and her husband had raised their grandson after the death of his parents—they had been strict with Barton at times, but he had never doubted their deep love for him. After his grandfather died, when Barton came of age, Lady Augusta had continued to live in Barton's home in the country rather than move to the Dower house. The affection and trust between Barton and Augusta was such that Barton left his estate affairs in his grandmother's hands when he was away.

Barton rose, smiling, when he saw his grandmother; his smile faded when he noticed that she had the morning's newspaper tucked under her arm.

"Yes, well may you look queasy," Lady Augusta snapped. "What is the meaning of this, sir? Answer me!'' She punctuated her words by rapping her cane sharply against the floor.

"Grandmama, I . . .'' Barton began.

"I am speaking, my lord,'' Augusta said coldly.

Despite himself, Barton's lips twitched. "My apologies, ma'am.''

"I am so glad that you find this all a source of amusement,'' Augusta drawled sarcastically. "Perhaps my sense of the absurd is deficient. When I read in the newspaper—the newspaper!—that my only grandson was wed, and to some chit I'd never even met, I must allow, laughter was the farthest thing from my mind.'' She met Barton's gaze, and he saw the genuine hurt in her bright blue eyes, so like his own.

"I am sorry,'' Barton said gently. "I never meant for you to learn of it in this way, truly. I rode hell for leather for two days to get here in time to tell you myself, but unfortunately, I dared not wait to send the announcement to the newspapers.'' Barton held out a hand to help his grandmother into a chair, but Augusta angrily shook her arm free.

"You shan't charm me, my boy,'' she said. "This is not some prank you've indulged in with those mutton-headed friends of yours—this is your life, and the future of your family. How did it happen, Barton? How?''

"You won't like it, Grandmama,'' Barton warned her.

"I don't like it now!'' she retorted.

With no further preamble, Lord Barton launched into the story of what had occurred on board the *Cumberland Rover*. It took only a few minutes to tell.

He finished by saying, "You do see why I sent the notice out immediately rather than waiting until after I told you, don't you?"

Augusta ignored his question. "How could you be so stupid, Barton?" she asked. "To be trapped so easily!"

"What could I do, Grandmama?"

"You should have thought of something," she told him dourly. "Lord knows, you've proven yourself clever enough at avoiding matrimony in the past."

"I might have managed the thing again had Amanda not been kin to General Stratton," Barton said. "You must admit, that did complicate the whole matter enormously."

Augusta's expression softened. "Your grandfather loved the general like a brother," she said. "There was no one he was closer to."

"I remember," Barton said. "Frankly, I wish I did not!" he added wryly.

"Well, I suppose that there is no use in crying over spilt milk," Lady Augusta said practically. She darted a shrewd glance at her grandson. "What's the chit like?"

Unbidden, a picture of Amanda, standing before the fireplace in her nightdress, rose before Barton's eyes. "I hardly know," he said, frowning.

Augusta, watching him closely, said acerbically, "I can see that she is attractive, at least. Else you would not be so easily reconciled to your fate!"

Stung, Barton retorted, "You could not be more wrong. I did what my honour demanded, but no more than that. Truth to tell, I can hardly bear to be in the same room with my esteemed wife."

Augusta snorted, a most unladylike sound.

"My only consolation," Barton continued, ignoring his grandmother's sceptical expression, "is that her lineage is good. It is some comfort that I shall have no reason to blush for my wife's family."

"I should not be so sure of that if I were you," Augusta prophesied darkly. "Have you met her uncle Cecil?"

Barton grimaced. "I've had that pleasure," he said ironically.

"Then you know that a more thorough wastrel you will never meet! As a boy he was a ne'er-do-well, and as a man he's worse. Your grandfather and I used to wonder how such a scoundrel could have sprung from the loins of one so worthy as the general. Be on your guard, Barton! Cecil will try to take advantage of your marriage to his niece."

"He'll be wasting his time if he does," Barton promised grimly. "Cecil Stratton shall get nothing from me, of that you may be sure."

"We shall see," Lady Augusta said. She rose slowly and crossed the room to tug at the bell-pull. "I'll have my maid begin packing immediately," she said. "We can leave for London in the morning."

Barton hesitated for a moment, then said, "Is it really a good time to come for a visit, Grandmama? I mean . . . as little as I may like it, Amanda is my wife! Are you sure you'll be able to control your indignation enough to be civil to her?"

"Do you dare to lecture me on my comportment, Barton?" Lady Augusta asked coldly.

"No, Grandmama," Barton said humbly, feeling suddenly very much the errant schoolboy.

"Good," his grandmother said. "My interest is strictly in squelching the gossip that this hasty marriage must be causing. If I come to stay with you, and can manage to appear pleased with the match, then the rumour-mongers may lose interest and move on to some other scandal."

"Thank you, my lady," Barton said with an engaging grin.

"You needn't thank me, scamp," Lady Augusta said. "I am as much a Barton as you are, and I shall not allow this creature you've married to drag our name into the mud. She may have thought herself home free once she had your ring on her finger, but the new Lady Barton has much to learn about being a true lady. And I," said Augusta, with a martial light in her eyes, "am just the person to teach her!"

THE RAVEN-HAIRED WOMAN slammed the town house door behind her. "Mavis!" she called. "Where are you?"

The maid hurried down the stairs. "Lady Travers!" she exclaimed. "We weren't expecting you until next week." She did not appear pleased to see her mistress.

Carolyn Travers pulled off her gloves with an impatient jerk, then removed her furs and tossed them carelessly towards a chair. "The country was simply too fatiguing," she said as she moved up the stairs.

"The duke promised me an amusing time, but it turned out that the only other guests there were all as old as he is, and every bit as tiresome. I dare say he thought he might bore me into his bed if he could not cajole me there! I endured it for as long as I could, but..." She shrugged prettily. "I was in such a hurry to leave that I didn't even stop to pack," she said. "My abigail will be arriving sometime tomorrow with all my things."

Mavis, the upstairs maid, scooped up the furs from the floor and trailed along in her mistress's wake as Carolyn moved up the stairs to the drawing-room. On a polished table, Carolyn found a pile of invitations and correspondence; she leafed through them quickly, and a small frown marred the perfect skin of her forehead. "Nothing from Lord Barton?" she said.

"No... no, madam," Mavis mumbled.

"Indeed," Carolyn purred. "What a naughty, naughty man he is, to be sure!"

"Maybe his lordship isn't back yet," the maid suggested, without looking at Carolyn. "He could be still in France."

"Oh, he's back," Carolyn said. "He'd never miss quarter day—Barton has a ridiculously overblown sense of responsibility to his tenants." She tapped one slender forefinger against her chin. "Perhaps he hasn't come because he heard that I was out of Town," she mused. "I hope so! After that ridiculous scene before he left, he would be well served indeed by a little jealous suffering."

Carolyn's cheeks reddened at the thought of that last encounter with Barton, right before he left for

France. How coolly he had told her that their relationship was finished, and how adroitly he had used those magnificent emeralds to distract her for long enough to make his escape! He would pay for that, Carolyn vowed silently.

"My lady…?" Mavis ventured hesitantly. "Did his lordship not say…I mean, did he not tell you…" Her voice faltered when Carolyn turned to look at her coldly.

"Do not overstep the bounds, Mavis," she said. "I may choose to talk to you from time to time, but pray do remember your place."

"Yes, madam." Mavis dropped her eyes.

"And if you were about to remind me that Barton gave me my *congé,* then you are even more foolish than I imagined," Carolyn said crushingly. "Barton was angry with me—for what reason I haven't the vaguest notion!—and he said some very foolish things, I'll grant you. But it meant nothing. I have absolutely no doubt that he will appear on my doorstep at any moment, begging me to forgive him." She smiled, a deep, sensual smile that made her green eyes look deceptively sleepy. "He won't be able to stop himself, you see," she added, and chuckled wickedly. "Yes, my lord Barton will come back, make no mistake about it. And when he does, we shall be as close as ever. In fact—" Carolyn's lips curled in a complacent smile "—in fact, it may very well be that we shall soon be more than close. I've decided that Barton might make me a very good husband."

Mavis opened her mouth soundlessly.

Carolyn glanced at Mavis lazily. "Why so surprised?"

"It's just that you've never seemed interested in marrying again, my lady," Mavis said weakly. "You've always been a lady as values her freedom."

Carolyn shrugged again. "I was," she admitted. "But it's begun to occur to me of late that it might be time for me to settle down."

Carolyn had not come to this conclusion lightly. Widowed at an early age after a brief marriage to an elderly sporting peer, and left with a respectable fortune, she had always considered that she had no reason to once more step into parson's mousetrap and subject herself to the vagaries of some gentleman's whims. Barton had made her rethink her opinion.

Carolyn's fortune was adequate; it allowed her to live in comfort and to afford the elegancies of life, if not its extravagancies. But Barton's fortune was enormous and, since becoming his mistress, Carolyn had tasted the luxury that was afforded by truly great wealth. It was a taste very much to her liking.

And Carolyn had noticed the way that the milk-and-water misses of Society pursued Barton. They set elaborate traps for him, eager to drag the ton's richest bachelor to the altar. Carolyn had begun to day-dream about how satisfying it would be to be presented to the ton as Lady Barton, and to laugh in the faces of all those virtuous young ladies who had once looked down their noses at her.

But most of all, Carolyn had come to believe that Barton's most useful bride gift to her would be security. If she continued her present mode of life, sooner or later she would be involved in some scandal that would be too great for the ton to ignore. They would shrug, brand her "not quite the thing," and turn their backs on Carolyn forever. But if she were Barton's wife, she would be absolutely safe. No scandal short of dalliance with a married Royal would be great enough to touch her; the Barton name was so old and respected that it would, Carolyn reckoned, cover a multitude of sins.

"I realize that Barton will not be easy to win," Carolyn continued briskly. "But I do believe that I'm equal to the task." She smiled at herself in a gilt-framed mirror, more than satisfied with what she saw.

"You can't marry him!" When Carolyn swung round to regard Mavis with narrowed eyes, the maid-servant clapped both hands over her mouth.

"Why not?" Carolyn asked sharply. "Why would you say such a thing?"

"My lady, I..." the maid squeaked. "It's not possible...you don't know...!" She pulled a folded news-sheet out of her deep apron pocket, thrust it at her mistress, then fled the room.

Carolyn stared after her servant, amazed by the woman's precipitate departure. Her eyes fell to the newspaper in her hand, and she sank into a chair as she read it.

Mavis, hurrying through the foyer, shook her head as she heard the shriek from the drawing-room echoing down the stairs. "There'll be the devil to pay," she prophesied darkly, "and no pitch hot!"

Carolyn sat bolt upright in her chair, the paper clutched between her rigid hands. "This cannot be,"

she said aloud. "It simply cannot be!" Once more she
reread the brief paragraph; there was no mistake.
William, Lord Barton was married. Carolyn crumpled up the news-sheet and hurled it towards the fireplace.

So much for her dreams of wedded bliss, Carolyn
thought bitterly. She wondered who this Amanda
Stratton was...and how the chit had managed to catch
Barton, for he was notoriously skilled at evading
matrimony. The girl must be a fast worker, too; Barton had only been out of London for six or seven
weeks, and he could not have been courting this
Stratton female before he left, else she would have
heard of it. It didn't matter, she decided. Whatever
had caused Barton to suddenly decide to wed, he had
not married Carolyn, and that, she supposed, ended
her interest in him.

Or did it? Her lips lifted in a hateful smile. This
Amanda Stratton had stolen from Carolyn social
prominence, untold wealth and the security of a
prominent name. What could be more just than if
Carolyn were to steal Barton back from the girl in return? Oh, he would never divorce the chit, that was
certain, but it might be that Carolyn could make his
wife's victory an empty one by seducing Barton back
into his old relationship with her. That done, she
would make quite sure that the new Lady Barton knew
all the sordid details of her husband's affair, and that
the girl reaped every bit of the humiliation she deserved.

Carolyn rose from her seat, her good humour
largely restored. Amanda Stratton might have won the

first battle, but she would not, Carolyn vowed, win the war!

THE BUTLER POURED a cup of coffee, set the newspapers at his master's elbow and bowed himself out. The dining-room was very quiet, the only sounds the ticking of the ornate clock on the mantel and the gentle click of spoon against cup as the man stirred milk into his coffee. Though the sun shone brightly outside, the curtains were drawn and candles gleamed at either end of the long table.

The Vicomte DeValme took a sip of his coffee and frowned thoughtfully at the newspaper before him. His fair, almost white hair and pale eyes gleamed in the candlelight; the rich black silk of his dressing-gown made his ashen skin appear all the more pallid by comparison. DeValme looked up as footsteps sounded on the marble floor, echoing in the stillness. He watched, expressionless, as his house guest crossed the dining-room and slid into the place set halfway down the long table.

"You're back," DeValme said, folding the paper up neatly. "When did you return?"

"Last night," Cecil Stratton mumbled. "Very late." He fumbled with his napkin. "I...I didn't wish to disturb you."

"How very thoughtful of you, Cecil," the *vicomte* said. "And your mission—it was successful?"

Cecil squirmed in his seat. "Well, no," he admitted reluctantly. "But I'll find her, never fear. She can't have gone far!"

DeValme leaned back in his chair, his fingers tapping gently against the side of his cup. "She may have gone rather farther than you think, *mon vieux*."

Cecil shook his head, the expression on his round face mulish. "It isn't possible. Amanda doesn't know a soul in France, and she hasn't a sou to call her own. I shall find her very soon, I know it. And you mustn't think that I shan't scold her—I shall be very firm with her, I promise you. Of course, as soon as she's back, the wedding can take place."

DeValme slapped the newspaper down before Cecil. "The wedding," he said, "has already taken place!"

Cecil Stratton read the short piece that DeValme pointed to with dismay. His pudgy hands shook as he put the paper down. "But...but..." he stammered.

"Yes, it is a bit of a shock, isn't it?" DeValme said silkily. "Our little Amanda, wed to my Lord Barton. I would almost believe that you were part of this—"

"No! No, I wasn't!" Cecil interrupted frantically. "I didn't know anything about it, I swear!"

"...did I not know what an arrant coward you are," DeValme finished. "You would never have the stomach to cross me, would you, Cecil?" DeValme regarded Amanda's uncle with contempt.

In truth, Cecil's craven nature had been one of the factors that had decided DeValme to marry Amanda. Scion of an old, illustrious and immensely wealthy French family, he was known far and wide as a base and evil man, his only interest the fulfilment of his own pleasures. *L'Ange infame* took what he wanted, be it woman, sport or revenge, and woe to anyone who tried to stand in his way.

When DeValme had decided that it was time for him to marry and beget an heir, he had discovered that no lady of birth in either France or England would consider his suit. Not the most rapacious of mamas, determined to marry her daughter to a fortune, would consider DeValme as a suitor, for what parent could knowingly give her child to a devil? DeValme had found the situation immensely galling; he considered himself, by virtue of his birth and fortune, to be above the conventions that ruled the rest of Society, and thought it presumptuous of any to dare judge his behaviour.

But no amount of scorn or anger had found DeValme a bride. It was unthinkable, of course, that he should marry out of his own class; he had been seriously considering the idea of simply kidnapping some likely young lady and marrying her out of hand when he had met Cecil Stratton. Cecil, in his cups one evening, had mentioned his ward, a young lady who had been raised almost entirely in the most secluded of circumstances. DeValme had found the thought of Amanda's innocence extremely piquant. To a palate as jaded as his, the notion of a fresh, young English girl had been very appealing. The knowledge that he might treat Cecil's niece as he wished, with no chance that Cecil would ever object, had finally decided DeValme to honour Amanda with his name.

"Still," DeValme continued, delicately sipping his coffee, "it does leave you in an interesting position, does it not, Cecil?"

"How . . . how do you mean?"

"You owe me a great deal of money, my friend, money that I loaned you in expectation of making your niece my wife. Are you prepared to repay me?"

Cecil blanched. "I cannot," he said. "You know I cannot!"

"I do hold your vowels, you'll recall," DeValme said. "I am quite determined to redeem them—one way or another." The implied threat was not lost on Cecil; DeValme was considered to be a deadly opponent on the field of honour. "And then there is the matter of the slur to my character."

"Now, that is beyond the limit," Cecil burst out. "Your character is already . . ."

DeValme met Cecil's eyes. "Yes?" he enquired gently.

Cecil stopped, swallowed and was silent.

"As I was saying," DeValme went on, "your niece has insulted me. By her precipitate flight, she has made it seem that any fate would be preferable to marriage with me. It won't do, I'm afraid."

"You can't blame me for that," Cecil protested. "Dash it all, I did everything I could to make her wed you!" Cecil looked into DeValme's face, and what he saw there made him grow even more pale. "I'll pay you back the money," he babbled. "You may rely on me, DeValme."

The *vicomte* quirked an eyebrow at his guest. "If you have demonstrated nothing else in your time here, Cecil, you have conclusively proven that you are the most unreliable of men."

Cecil was thinking. "I'll get the money from Amanda!" he said. "This Barton is said to be a warm 'un, and it's only right that Amanda should make amends for all the trouble she's caused."

DeValme laughed. "I doubt she will see it that way," he said. "I dare say she'll send you on your way with a flea in your ear and count herself well rid of her loving uncle."

Cecil's face took on a cunning look. "I could make London very uncomfortable for her," he said. "If the news of her disgraceful flight from France were to be bruited about, she'd be a social outcast. I have no doubt that she'll pay, to keep her secrets."

"Bravo, Cecil!" DeValme said, not entirely without admiration. "You do not hesitate, do you, to throw her to the wolves?"

"She deserves nothing better," Cecil said sulkily. "It's all her own fault."

"So it is, *mon vieux,* so it is," DeValme agreed.

"I'll leave for England today," Cecil went on, not looking at DeValme. "I'll be back as soon as I have the money."

"No need," DeValme said expansively.

"You're quite right, of course, DeValme," Cecil said heartily. "I can simply send you a bank draft, can't I?"

"You misunderstand me, Cecil," DeValme said. "Can you think that I am so foolish as to let you out of my sight before you've paid me? You would never return, and then I should be put to the trouble of hunting you down and killing you. A tiresome prospect, you'll agree? No, I believe I shall accompany you to England."

"There's no reason . . ." Cecil began.

"But there is every reason," DeValme contradicted him. "You see, money is not the only thing that Lord and Lady Barton owe me." He suddenly looked every inch *l'Ange infame.* "They owe me revenge, and I shall have it. I assure you, my dear Cecil, I shall have it!"

CHAPTER FIVE

CHAS WENDOVER RAPPED on the door of Barton's house in Grosvenor Square, barely able to contain his impatience. He waited a moment, sighed irascibly, then lifted his cane to knock again just as the door opened before him.

"Good Lord, Dennison, what took you so long?" he complained as he stepped inside. "I've been banging on the door for ten minutes!"

Barton's butler did not appear much chastened by Chas's sharp comment. "I was otherwise engaged, sir," he said.

Chas's scepticism was evident, but he said only "Where is Lady Barton?"

"The young lady is having her breakfast," the servant replied with a sniff.

Charles froze. "The young lady?" he repeated in an awful tone.

"Her ladyship, that is to say," Dennison corrected himself sullenly.

Chas fixed the butler with a cold stare. "You would do well to remember," he said, "that Lady Barton is now mistress of this house. I would be most distressed to hear that she had not been accorded every courtesy due to her, as would Lord Barton—most distressed indeed. Do I make myself clear?''

Dennison nodded, his pasty skin mottled with patches of angry colour. He crossed the foyer to reopen the outer door. "Shall I tell *her ladyship*—'' he stressed the words "—that you will return later, sir?''

"Not at all,'' Chas said, calmly depositing his hat and cane on a table. "I'm quite sure that Lady Barton will not mind if I join her for breakfast. No need to show me the way, Dennison. I am quite familiar with the household.'' He smiled at the servant, but it was not a friendly smile. "You would do well to remember it.'' Barton's friend turned and ran lightly up the stairs.

Chas shook his head as he strode down the hall towards the dining-room. The insolence of the butler amazed him, but he supposed it was only to be expected. Barton's surprise marriage had been bound to cause talk among the staff; his even more surprising departure the morning after the ceremony was a signal to anyone with wits that there was something havey-cavey going on. And an opportunist like Dennison would need no more than a hint that there was something amiss to take liberties. Chas hoped that the servant had not been making Amanda too unhappy.

Chas had become very fond of Amanda during the past week. He had appointed himself her companion while Barton was gone; he had called on her every day and done his best to keep her amused. Chas's initial impression of Barton's wife had been confirmed, at least to his satisfaction—he found Amanda to be a quiet, well-bred young lady, caught up, through no fault of her own, in a terrible situation.

Chas reached the dining-room and looked through the open double doors before entering. Amanda was sitting at the end of the long table, staring down into a cup of tea. Her expression was unhappy; the circles under her eyes indicated that she had not been sleeping well. Chas determinedly set his lips in a smile and stepped into the room.

"Good morning, fair one!" he said. "I've come to join you for breakfast, if you don't object?"

Amanda looked up. Chas was flattered but saddened by the brilliant smile that lit her face. "Chas!" she exclaimed. "Come in, come in—let me make you a plate." Despite Chas's protestations that there was no need for her to wait on him, Amanda insisted he seat himself and allow her to bring him a selection from the serving dishes on the sideboard.

"You are indeed my good angel, for I was just sitting here indulging in a fit of the megrims," Amanda said as she set the heaping plate before him. "I was never so glad to see anyone!"

"I don't doubt it for a moment," Chas said, round a mouthful of coddled eggs. "Lord, but it's a gloomy place!" He indicated the echoing, dark-panelled dining-room with a wave of his fork. "It's no wonder you're blue-devilled, having your meals all alone in this great barn of a room."

"It is rather...lonely," Amanda agreed wistfully. "And the food arrives shockingly cold—it's such a long way from the kitchens, you see. I have been thinking that there must be some other room in this

enormous house where one could dine in more pleasant surroundings, but Dennison says that Lord Barton always has his meals served here," Amanda said,
her eyes fixed on her plate. Chas noticed that she was
not eating.

"Well, tell Dennison that *you* don't care to," Chas
said cheerfully. "We can't have you wasting away to
nothing over something so foolish."

"Truth to tell," Amanda responded, "I am not
certain that Dennison would pay any heed to my
wishes if I did."

"He had dashed well better!" Chas exclaimed. "It's
high time that someone reminded Dennison that he is
only a servant in this house." He shook his head. "I
can't think why Barton hasn't shown him the door by
now. He's an insolent clod, and a terrible butler to
boot."

"I have not found him to be very easy to deal with,"
Amanda admitted. "Mrs. Mandley, the housekeeper,
has been very kind, and the other servants are not un-
friendly, but Dennison . . . !" She shrugged helplessly.

"You must be more strict with him, Amanda,"
Chas said gently. "Dennison's attitude towards you is
intolerable. He should be doing your bidding, not you
his."

"I have no right to order Barton's servants about,"
Amanda said.

"No one has a better right!" Chas said. "You are
Lady Barton, and mistress of this house. Everything
should be ordered to your satisfaction. Bart would
agree with me, I know, if he were here."

Amanda met Chas's gaze. "But he isn't here, is he?" she said quietly. "And that tells Dennison, and the other servants, all they need to know about the nature of our marriage. Dennison's lack of respect towards me merely mirrors his master's opinion." She essayed a shaky smile. "And, on a more practical level, I doubt if Barton would thank me for oversetting his household arrangements in his absence."

Chas looked at Amanda consideringly. "On the contrary, I think that Barton would be most grateful if you could set the running of this house to rights. You must have seen by now how shockingly Barton's servants use him. This entire establishment is ordered for the convenience of the servants rather than the comfort of its master."

"That is certainly true," Amanda agreed. "Mrs. Mandley is a dear, but far too soft-hearted to discipline the staff as she should. The housemaids have become incredibly lazy! You would not credit the dust that lies about this house—truly, Chas, you wouldn't."

"So you see, you would actually be doing Bart a service if you could take the staff in hand," Chas said persuasively. "Good God, Amanda, think of the food alone—I vow, Bart has the worst cook in London."

"I noticed!" Amanda said, a twinkle in her eye. Her expression sobered. "Do you really think that I could be of help?"

"I'm sure of it," Chas said enthusiastically.

"It would be nice to have something to do," Amanda admitted wistfully. "As you know, Chas, I was accustomed to being busy, when I was at Miss

Hagstrom's. The time has been hanging heavily on my hands, I must allow."

"I've done my level best to keep you amused, my dear!"

"Oh, Chas, you've been wonderful," Amanda said with a warm smile. "I don't know what I should have done if you hadn't come to call every day. You are such a good friend!"

Chas was touched. "Nonsense, Amanda, it has been my pleasure, I promise you. And Bart will be back soon."

"Will he? I wonder."

"Of course he will," Chas said firmly. He hesitated for a moment, then went on, "You must try to understand why he went. Bart is remarkably close to Lady Augusta. He could not just allow her to read of his marriage in the newspaper. He had to go and explain...what happened."

"How I stalked and trapped him into marriage? An edifying tale," Amanda said wryly. "I have no doubt that Lady Augusta will be looking forward to making my acquaintance with great anticipation."

"Oh, I shouldn't worry about Lady Augusta if I were you," Chas said, pretending to a confidence he did not feel. "She's a wily old thing. She'll see what kind of person you are in a wink, and then you two shall deal remarkably well."

"I only hope that you may prove to be right!" Amanda said, trying to hide her anxiety from Chas.

The butler re-entered the dining-room. Chas leaned over and said to Amanda, "No time like the present, my dear."

Amanda took a deep breath, then said, "Dennison, starting with luncheon today, you will serve all meals in the ... the ..." She looked at Chas blankly.

"The morning-room," he supplied helpfully.

"The morning-room," Amanda continued, with a grateful smile for Chas. "Is that quite clear?"

"But Lord Barton ..." the butler began.

"Lord Barton will be quite pleased with the change, I have no doubt," Amanda said firmly.

The butler opened his mouth, but when he saw Chas's challenging stare, he closed it again.

"Yes, Dennison?" Amanda asked. "Is there anything else?"

"A Mr. Stratton to see you, mi—my lady," the butler said, sliding a resentful glance at Chas. "A Mr. Cecil Stratton."

The colour drained from Amanda's face so quickly that, for a moment, Chas thought she might actually faint.

Chas covered her hand with his own. "Amanda?" he asked. "Are you all right?" Amanda nodded. "You don't have to see him, you know," Chas added softly.

"I'm sure that Uncle Cecil came to London expressly to visit me," Amanda said. "He's a very stubborn man. He won't leave until he has the chance to call on me." Amanda smiled weakly. "You were quite right—there is no time like the present." To Dennison, she said, "Give us a moment, then show Mr. Stratton into the drawing-room, please." She pushed back her chair, looking for all the world, Chas thought sympathetically, as if she were about to face the gallows.

Amanda and Chas had just settled themselves in the drawing-room when Dennison ushered Cecil Stratton in.

"Good morning, Uncle Cecil," Amanda said, rising to her feet. "I trust you had a good journey?"

"I'm surprised that you have the stomach to face me after the way you've behaved," Cecil Stratton said, his round face set in a scowl. "I never should have thought that you would prove yourself to be such an ungrateful, unnatural..."

"Ahem." Chas cleared his throat and rose from the wing-chair that had hidden him from Cecil's view.

The scowl was instantly wiped from Cecil's face, to be replaced by a broad, obsequious smile. "My lord Barton, I presume?" he said, holding out his hand. "How good to finally meet you, my lord."

"Uncle Cecil, this is Chas Wendover," Amanda said hastily. "He is a new friend. He has been most kind to me since I came to Town."

"Indeed?" Cecil said, his scowl returning.

Chas nodded infinitesimally. "Mr. Stratton," he acknowledged. He did not smile.

"I'm sure that you will forgive me, Mr. Wendover, if I tell you that I am most desirous of speaking to my niece in private. You will excuse us?"

Chas looked to Amanda. "Would you like me to stay?" he asked softly.

Amanda shook her head. "I shall be fine," she said. "Truly, Chas. And thank you for joining me for breakfast!"

"As you wish, then," Chas said, and bowed over her hand. "Your servant, sir," he said stiffly to Cecil, and was gone.

Cecil Stratton raised his quizzing glass and stared after the departed Chas. "What a very peculiar young man, to be sure," he said.

"There is nothing the least bit peculiar about him," Amanda said, bridling. "He is one of the kindest, most thoughtful people I've ever met."

"In my day," Cecil said with a sniff, "a young gentleman did not dally alone with a married woman, over breakfast or any other meal. I fear that manners have greatly changed since I was last in London."

"On the contrary, manners have not changed at all," Amanda retorted. "It would be a sad day indeed when my lord Barton's closest friend was not welcome in his home."

Cecil went on as though Amanda had not spoken. "Still, it's no more than I've come to expect from you, Amanda. I've learned, to my sorrow, what freakish starts you are capable of."

"If you are referring to my return to England..."

"Your return to England—how delicately put, my dear. You might say, rather, your heedless flight from your legal guardian, or your blind refusal to submit yourself to the judgement of older and wiser heads— or even your hoydenish escapades across the length and breadth of France!" Cecil was very angry.

"I did what I had to do," Amanda said. "What you forced me to do, Uncle!"

"I forced you to behave like the veriest light skirt? I forced you to run to Barton like a mare in heat? I think not," Cecil said coldly.

"You forced me to run away," Amanda burst out, "by trying to compel me to marry DeValme!"

"The *vicomte* would have made a very good match for you, Amanda," Cecil said. "Far better than you deserve, in point of fact."

"Have you so black an opinion of my character, then, that you would mate me to *l'Ange infame?* The man is a scoundrel!"

Cecil shrugged. "You would do well to learn not to listen to gossip. A true lady would not soil her ears with the kind of nonsense that is spoken of De-Valme."

"Nonsense, you call it? I'm sure that Lady Heth-roe would not call it so—was it not her daughter who put a period to her existence after being compromised by DeValme? And what of poor Lord Donner? Eighteen years old the boy was, and DeValme slew him on the duelling field, only because Donner said that he did not care for DeValme's waistcoat. Think of it, Uncle—the boy died because he did not like the work of DeValme's tailor!"

"DeValme did design the waistcoat himself," Cecil pointed out. Amanda only stared at him. "At any rate," he mumbled, "those were isolated occurrences—both of them."

"I could name you a dozen more such incidents, did I think that you would listen," Amanda said bitterly. "And if I, living in my quiet backwater of a school, have heard so much evil of DeValme, one can only

shudder to think of his true infamy, if all were
known!" Amanda turned away from Cecil in disgust.
"Are you so blinded by his fortune that you cannot see
what he is?" she asked. "Or can it be, dear Uncle, that
you simply don't care?"

"How dare you speak to me so, you ungrateful
chit?" Cecil hissed. "Have you any idea how much
trouble you've caused me?"

"I have no doubt that DeValme is displeased..."
Amanda began.

"Displeased?" Cecil exclaimed. "This is a man who
would kill over a waistcoat! I must assure you, madam, that I shall not face DeValme's anger alone when
you are the sole cause of it. You shall make it right,
Amanda."

"It is a little late for that, Uncle Cecil," Amanda
said, suddenly tired. "However angry DeValme may
be, there is no way that I can make it right, as you say.
I am already married to Lord Barton."

"Yes," Cecil said. He looked around the opulent
drawing-room. "And you have done very well for
yourself, by the look of it. Perhaps you are more clever
than I had imagined."

Amanda burned with shame. No wonder Barton
thought she had married him for his fortune if even
her own uncle believed it!

"It is as well that Barton is well-heeled," Cecil
continued. "For there is still the little matter of the
money that we owe to DeValme."

"What money?" Amanda asked suspiciously. "I
certainly don't recall borrowing any money from
him."

"I borrowed it, in expectation of your future nuptials," Cecil said smoothly. "Now, of course, De-Valme wants it back." Cecil swung round to face Amanda. "And you, my dear girl, shall give it to me."

Amanda gasped. "I will not," she said. "And why should I? I never saw a groat of it. You never so much as bought me a new frock!"

Cecil seized Amanda by the arm, squeezing it cruelly. "This is all your fault, my dear niece, and you shall make it right. You shall, or I'll..."

What Cecil would do remained a mystery, as at that moment the drawing-room door opened. Cecil immediately released Amanda's arm and moved away from his niece.

Lady Augusta Barton stepped into the room, her grandson just behind her. The dowager was wrapped in a black travelling cloak. Though her back was as straight as ever, she leaned heavily on her cane, and dark circles under her eyes revealed her exhaustion. "Ah," she said, her tone withering. She shot a triumphant look at Barton. "I see that you've wasted no time in joining your niece, Stratton."

Cecil Stratton bowed low, his face wreathed in smiles. "How flattered I am that you remember me, my lady," he said. "It must be almost twenty years since last we saw each other!"

"You haven't changed much," Augusta said. "A little stouter, perhaps, and a great deal more florid, but fundamentally the same." Her voice dripped scorn. "You remember my grandson, Barton, I'm sure," Augusta added.

Barton and Cecil exchanged stiff bows, then Barton said, "Grandmama, this is my wife, Amanda." His tone was heavy with irony. "Amanda, this is is my grandmother, Lady Augusta Barton."

Amanda curtseyed, then looked up to find herself fixed by a pair of piercing blue eyes. Augusta lifted her lorgnette and slowly looked Amanda up and down. The girl's quiet green morning frock was unexceptionable, Augusta was bound to admit, and at least the creature didn't paint! "Well," she said grudgingly, "you aren't as bad as I feared you might be, at any rate."

Angry colour rose in Amanda's cheeks. "How kind of you to say so, ma'am," she answered coldly.

"Amanda!" Barton snapped.

So, Augusta thought, *this cat has claws, does she?* "It *was* kind of me, girl," she said. "I could have said much worse, could I not?"

Cecil looked back and forth from Augusta to Amanda, then cleared his throat. "I dare say you're all wishing me at the devil." he said. "A quiet family cose is what you want, and I am sadly *de trop,* I fear. I shall say goodbye. Amanda, remember what I told you," he added. "Good day, all!" He bowed and left the drawing-room hastily.

"What an intolerable mushroom that man is," Augusta said to Barton. She sighed. "Your grandfather would turn over in his grave to see that rogue a part of our family, however distantly."

Amanda's anger drained away. Why should Lady Augusta not despise her? she asked herself tiredly. All that the dowager knew of her was that she had trapped

Barton into marriage and that she was related to Cecil Stratton, who was, Amanda privately thought, far worse than a mushroom!

"You have a great deal to answer for, miss," Augusta said, breaking into Amanda's thoughts. "You may have thought yourself fallen into the honey-pot, my girl, but you may find the reality to be very much inferior to the dream!"

Amanda lifted her head proudly and met Lady Augusta's gaze. "You are very much mistaken, my lady, if you believe that this marriage is any more to my liking than it is to yours," she said quietly. "I promise you, it is not."

"That," the elderly lady said obscurely, "remains to be seen!" She seemed suddenly to realize that she was still standing in the middle of the drawing-room. "What are you thinking of, Barton?" she asked crossly, rapping her cane sharply against the floor. "Do you keep all your guests standing about in their wraps, or is that a treat reserved specially for me?"

"You did insist on coming directly upstairs," Barton reminded her, half smiling. "You wouldn't allow Dennison to take your cloak, if you'll recall."

"And why anyone would give anything to that whey-faced, pitiful excuse for a butler, I don't know," Augusta said. "If the rest of your staff is as sorry as he is, my stay here will be a short one, Barton!"

"I am suitably chastened, I assure you, Grandmama," Barton said with a grin. He took Augusta by the elbow. "Now I'll see you upstairs, and on the way, you may tell me at great length what an unsatisfactory grandson I am." He opened the door and assisted the dowager out of the drawing-room.

As Barton turned to close the door behind him, he caught a last glimpse of Amanda. Her defiant pride seemed to have deserted her; she stood with shoulders slumped and, as Barton watched, sank unsteadily into a chair. Suddenly, unexpectedly, the peer felt a twinge of sympathy for his bride, sitting so forlornly in the middle of the empty drawing-room.

CHAPTER SIX

AMANDA TOOK a deep breath and pressed her hands together in her lap. Unable to sit still, the girl jumped to her feet and began to move around the morning-room. Once again she checked to make sure the dishes on the sideboard were properly warmed, then she straightened the cutlery beside one of the three place settings at the table and moved the vase of flowers so that it was exactly centred on the polished mahogany. Amanda slid the chairs into a more precise arrangement before their places, rubbed at an imaginary spot on the table with her handkerchief, then hastily tucked the used linen away in her sleeve. Finally, satisfied, she sank back into her seat, only to wonder anew if the food were indeed warm enough....

The door to the morning-room flew open with a bang. Amanda jumped and recoiled slightly as Barton charged in. His jaw was rigid with anger, and he glared at Amanda.

Lady Augusta came in next, her blue eyes bright with interest. "Gently, Barton, gently," she said dampingly. "No Cheltenham tragedies if you please—at the very least, not before breakfast!"

The last one to enter the morning-room was Dennison. Amanda's heart sank as she saw the look of smug satisfaction on the butler's face.

"You have taken a great deal upon yourself, madam," Barton said, scowling.

Lady Augusta's eyes moved from Barton to Amanda. "That will be all, Dennison," she said sharply.

Barton had not taken his eyes from Amanda. "How dared you tell Dennison to serve us our meals here instead of in the dining-room?"

Amanda took a deep breath. "My lord, let me explain...."

"What is there to explain? After one week in this house, you have overset a custom that has held true here since my grandfather's time. From the time I was a boy we have eaten our meals in that dining-room. You had no right—"

His grandmother interrupted him. "I should like to hear what Amanda has to say about the change," she said. When Barton turned to her, Augusta raised one haughty eyebrow. "You've no objection, I assume, Barton?" Barton looked at Augusta for a moment. He opened his mouth to speak, closed it again, then shrugged.

"Thank you, my lady," Amanda said with a grateful, if surprised, smile for Augusta. "Truly, my lord, I had no intention of oversetting anything," she went on earnestly. "It only seemed to me that, since the morning-room is so much closer to the kitchens, the food might stay hotter if we dined here. And I thought that it might be more pleasant to eat in a smaller room, at least when we are dining *en famille.*"

Barton gave a rude snort. "Whatever we may be, we are far from being a family!"

"I am sorry, my lord," Amanda said quietly. "I shall tell Dennison..."

"Nonsense, girl," Augusta interrupted again, seating herself at the table. "Don't apologize—you're right."

"Grandmama..."

"Lord knows, I tried often enough to convince your grandfather of the very same thing, Barton," Augusta said. "That great barn of a dining-room was all very well when we were seating twenty or thirty to dinner, but for those times when we dined alone, I found it depressing in the extreme." Barton gaped at her as Augusta added, "Did you never wonder why I so often took my meals on a tray in my room? Your grandfather was an estimable gentleman, but at times he was too aware of his own consequence." She nodded at Amanda. "A very good notion, this change," she said approvingly.

"You are very kind, ma'am," Amanda said. She smiled at Augusta.

"Now," Augusta said briskly, "if you'll be so kind as to make me a plate, Barton? I'm quite famished."

"Shall I ring for Dennison, my lady?' Amanda asked.

"Heavens, no—I can't abide that oily-faced trickster," Augusta said. "I won't have him creeping round me before I've even broken my fast."

"Then let me do it," Amanda said eagerly, rising to her feet. She moved to the sideboard and set about choosing those titbits most likely to tempt an elderly woman's appetite.

"Grandmama, I should have thought that you would support me," Barton said, low-voiced.

"She was right and you were wrong," Augusta answered as quietly. "Wrong and, may I add, appallingly rude into the bargain!"

Amanda returned with Augusta's plate. "Here you are, my lady," she said, eager to please. "If there is anything else that you'd like . . . ?"

"This is fine," Augusta said. "Sit down, girl, do! I can't abide a restive female."

Amanda sat back down and nervously picked at her tea and toast. The room was very quiet; Barton had buried his head in a newspaper, and Augusta seemed content to eat in silence.

Dennison re-entered the morning-room. "A caller for you, Lady Barton," he said, his gaze fixed somewhere over Amanda's left shoulder.

"For me?" Amanda asked, surprised. The butler nodded. "But whom?"

Dennison seemed not to hear her question; he moved to the door and held it open expectantly. Amanda hesitated for a moment, then left the room.

As soon as the door closed behind her, Barton put down his paper. "How can you take her part?" he demanded of his grandmother. "She's turned my whole household topsy-turvy!"

"Don't be absurd," Augusta said. "Amanda has simply put right an error that should have been corrected long ago."

"She had no right..." Barton began.

"She had every right in the world—she is your wife, and mistress of this house," Augusta snapped. "It is too late to alter that fact! When you married Amanda, you made the smooth operation of this household her concern. She is doing no more than her duty by taking charge—and past time, too! These servants of yours, with the exception of Mrs. Mandley, have been riding roughshod over you for years."

"My servants are perfectly competent," Barton said stubbornly.

Augusta shook her head pityingly. "You've been ill-served for so long that you've forgotten what good servants are!" she said. "*They* haven't, though! Why do you think Dennison was so quick to tell you about Amanda's change of dining arrangements and so eager to put the worst possible face on it? I suspect that he is very much afraid that this new broom will indeed sweep clean, and brush him right out the door!" Augusta chuckled wickedly. "It would positively do my heart good to see Amanda set that loathsome man in his place."

"Why this sudden change of heart?" Barton asked suspiciously. "Not twenty-four hours ago you were referring to Amanda as a shameless jade!"

Lady Augusta looked troubled. "Truth to tell, she's not at all what I expected," she confessed. "I see a great deal more of the general in her than I had expected to, and it has me puzzled, I don't hesitate to own. Judging strictly by appearances, she seems just the sort of quiet, well-bred young woman that one might meet at Almack's.''

Barton threw his napkin down on the table in disgust and rose to leave. ''Need I remind you, Grandmama, that we did not meet at Almack's? Amanda's presence on board the *Cumberland Rover* tells us all we need to know about what sort of person she is.''

''Perhaps,'' Augusta acknowledged. ''And perhaps there is more to all this than meets the eye. I'll reserve judgement, for the moment at least.'' She fixed a shrewd gaze on her grandson and added, ''I suggest that you do the same!''

Barton left the morning-room fuming. Whoever would have thought that Amanda could breach Augusta's defences so easily? Barton strode along the hall angrily. Despite his grandmother's words about reserving judgement, Barton could see that she was not displeased with what she had seen of Amanda so far. *So much for family loyalty,* he thought.

Barton's pace slowed. His grandmother was remarkably shrewd as a rule. He had relied on her perspicacity a dozen times, and never regretted it. He was forced to face the possibility that perhaps—perhaps!—Augusta was right, and Amanda was not so terrible, after all. It was difficult for him to consider the notion; he was still too angry with his bride to think her possessed of a single good quality. Nevertheless, his anger had faded enough for him to realize that it was in both his and Amanda's best interests to find some way to rub along together tolerably. Scenes like this morning's could be avoided if only the two of them could come to some kind of truce for the future.

Barton was not one to postpone the unpleasant. If there was to be dialogue between him and Amanda, then it must be now. He made his way to the drawing-room, his step firm, and paused only to take a deep breath before quietly opening the door.

"...So, when I learned that some clever puss had finally put an end to his overlong bachelorhood I said, 'Depend upon it, my dears—this bride of Barton's must be something very special indeed!'" Carolyn Travers's clear tones rang out. "You can see why I felt compelled to hurry along and meet you."

Barton jerked to a stop, still hidden from the room by the half open door.

"If you'll take a bit of friendly advice from me, you won't pay too much mind to Barton's little ways," Carolyn continued. "He can be quite trying, particularly in the morning, but if you are sweet to him, I believe you'll find him to be quite manageable."

Barton stepped into the drawing-room, his face an impassive mask.

"And here he is now!" Carolyn said. Barton's former mistress glowed in russet silk, her dark hair loose about her face. She stepped towards him, holding out both hands so that Barton felt obliged to take them. "I call you the slyest thing in nature, Barton—keeping this pretty young thing your secret. Imagine, surprising us by presenting her as your wife! You are a naughty creature, to be sure." She smiled brilliantly at Barton, then turned back to Amanda. "You must know, Amanda—may I call you Amanda?—you must know, my dear, that Barton and I have been friends simply forever. Such adventures as we have had!'' Carolyn slanted a provocative look at Barton.

One look at Amanda's unhappy expression told Barton that she well understood what Carolyn was so blatantly insinuating. "How good of you to call, Carolyn,'' he said, unsmiling. "I see that you have met Lady Barton.''

"Indeed I have, and she is charming, Bart, simply charming! I can well see why you so willingly stepped into parson's mousetrap.''

Amanda blushed hotly, and Carolyn's interest visibly quickened. "I do love a romantic tale,'' she said. "Tell me, Amanda—how did you two meet?''

Barton stepped to Amanda's side and took her arm casually in his. "I'm sure that my wife would like nothing better than to regale you with the story,'' Barton said blandly, "but she is engaged to go driving with Lady Augusta. Aren't you, pet?''

Carolyn stared at Amanda for a moment, her eyes narrowed, then reluctantly took up her furs and reticule. "I'll say good morning, then. And I must apologize again, my dear, for intruding,'' Carolyn said. "But I simply could not wait to offer you my felicitations.''

"I shall see you to your carriage, Carolyn,'' Barton said.

"Oh, there's no need ...''

"I insist,'' he said firmly and, taking Carolyn by the elbow, escorted her out of the room.

"Really, Barton, I don't think ...'' Carolyn began.

His grip on her arm unyielding, Barton led her along the hall, down the stairs and into his library. "What were you thinking of, Caro?" he asked as soon as the door was closed behind them.

"But how ungracious of you," Carolyn purred. She moved closer to Barton, so close that he could feel her breath on his cheek. "Won't you even say a proper hello to me, *chéri?*" She placed both her hands on his chest.

Barton stepped away from her. "What do you want?" he asked bluntly.

An angry light began to dance in Carolyn's eyes. "Be careful, Bart," she said. "You are on the verge of being positively offensive."

"It was a simple question, Caro," Barton replied. "Why did you come?"

"Why, to see her, of course," Carolyn answered disdainfully. "And I must say, I am disappointed! I never would have thought you'd settle for some milk-and-water miss with more hair than wit."

"My wife's wits are none of your concern, Caro," Barton said bluntly. "And I should prefer to keep it that way if you don't mind."

"Meaning?"

"Meaning," Barton said deliberately, "that I do not think it wise for you to pursue an acquaintance with my lady."

"I see," Carolyn said tightly. "In other words, I am not fit to associate with your dear Amanda?" Carolyn's anger burst into flame when Barton shrugged.

"So the little bride is too fine and pure for the likes of me, is she? Oh, Barton, you shall be sorry that you spoke to me so!"

"Do your worst, Carolyn," Barton said. "It is a matter of supreme indifference to me."

"We shall see how indifferent you are," Carolyn hissed, "when yours is the most gossiped about marriage in London!"

"Pray don't be absurd." Barton hid his apprehension. "As always, my dear, you've allowed your temper to overrun your good sense."

"Have I? It would be clear to the meanest intelligence that there's something havey-cavey about this match," Carolyn said as she yanked her gloves on. "I shall discover what it is and make it my business to tell the world. Will you be sorry then, I wonder?" Suddenly she stopped and stared at Barton. "Perhaps you won't be," she said slowly. "Did she trap you, Barton? Did little Miss Butter-wouldn't-melt-in-her-mouth land the biggest fish in the matrimonial sea?" She laughed aloud. "A clever puss, indeed!"

"We will not discuss Lady Barton any further, if you please," Barton said in the most haughty tone he could manage. "Her character would, of course, be incomprehensible to you."

Carolyn's fair skin reddened. "Not for long," she said, and pulled the library door open. "I shall learn everything there is to know about this bride of yours, Barton. And when I do, we shall see who is too good for whom!"

Barton groaned as the door slammed behind Carolyn. He crossed the room and dropped into the leather chair behind the desk, then barely stifled another groan as the door opened again.

Augusta came in, cane in hand. "What the devil is Dennison about?" she demanded.

Barton smiled. "Such language, Grandmama!" he teased.

"I've never been one to hide my teeth, you young scamp, and I shan't start now!" Lady Augusta replied. "And do not change the subject, if you please. What was Dennison thinking of, allowing that Travers woman into the house?"

Barton looked stunned; Augusta eyed her grandson with sardonic amusement. "Thought I didn't know she was your light o' love, didn't you? How excessively backward of you, Barton! I'm not some country cousin, I'll remind you. Despite my distance from London, I manage to hear what goes on in the world."

"How did you know that Lady Travers had been here?" Barton asked uncomfortably.

"I saw Amanda leaving the drawing-room looking as sick as a cat," Augusta answered. "The chit wouldn't say what was bothering her, though. Told me her breakfast didn't agree with her, as if she'd eaten more than a bite to begin with! So I sent for Dennison and asked who Amanda's caller had been. He tried to put me off, but I got it out of him in the end. And read him a thundering scold for it, too!"

"It was a mistake for Dennison to admit Carolyn, I'll grant you," Barton said. "But to be fair, he had never been told that Amanda was not at home to Carolyn."

"Nonsense," Lady Augusta scoffed. "Are you trying to tell me that Dennison didn't know of your relationship with the Travers woman? I don't believe it—servants know everything."

Barton did not answer; he realized that Dennison must have known about Carolyn, for Barton had brought her home once or twice for an intimate supper.

Augusta read his expression. "There, then!" she said triumphantly. "He knew. He only let la Travers see Amanda to cause trouble. Infamous—and impertinent! What do you intend to do about it?"

"I shall speak to him," Barton said.

Augusta snorted. "Just make sure that it is you who does the speaking," she said, "for of a certainty, he'll try to spin you a tale!" With that, she turned and stamped out of the library.

Barton sat for several minutes absently twirling his quizzing glass before he finally tugged on the bell-pull. When the butler entered the library, Barton motioned to him to shut the door behind him.

"Yes, my lord?"

"Sit down," Barton said evenly. The servant frowned and perched uncomfortably on the edge of a chair.

"Dennison, how long have you been with me now?"

"Almost four years, my lord," Dennison said smugly.

"And you have been happy in my employ? You've found me to be an equitable master?" Barton's tone was deceptively gentle.

"Oh, indeed, sir." The butler smiled obsequiously.

"Do you wish to continue as part of this household?" Barton fixed an icy gaze on Dennison, and the butler at last saw the anger in his employer's eyes.

Dennison started to speak, but Barton cut him off. "Do not waste my time or yours in attempting to defend the indefensible," he said. "You know that you should never have admitted Lady Travers to this house without informing me of her arrival. That you allowed her to see Lady Barton . . . !"

"I assumed that Lady Travers was a friend of her ladyship's," Dennison protested.

"You are surely aware that my wife has only recently come to Town," Barton said. "How, pray tell, would she know Carolyn?"

"Being unfamiliar with Lady Barton's background, I felt it would have been presumptuous of me to deny her to callers," Dennison said piously. "Her ladyship seems possessed of a broad range of acquaintances."

"Does she, now?"

"Her ladyship has had several visitors," Dennison said. "A Mr. Cecil Stratton has called, as well as Mr. Wendover." The butler slid a sly glance at his employer. "Indeed, Mr. Wendover has been most flattering in his attentions while you were away."

Barton remembered what Augusta had said. "Just what are you implying, Dennison?"

"Nothing, sir, nothing at all!"

"Let us have no misunderstandings here," Barton said. "I will not—" he emphasized every word "—I repeat, I will not tolerate the slightest hint of disrespect to Lady Barton. I should truly hate to let you go, Dennison, but that is what I will do should there be any repetition of this morning's events. And, since you appear to be in need of instruction in your duties, strive to remember this—you are not, under any circumstances, to admit Carolyn Travers to this house again. Do you understand?''

"I understand, my lord," Dennison said sullenly.

Barton nodded his dismissal and turned away. He did not see the angry resentment on his butler's face, or the dull gleam of hatred in the man's eyes.

As Dennison left the room, Barton did not realize that, without meaning to, he had gained Amanda yet another implacable enemy.

CHAPTER SEVEN

BARTON SAT before the bow window at White's club, absently watching the traffic in the street outside. His mood was gloomy; he could not recall, he thought darkly, when last a day had started so badly! First, there had been that scene with Amanda in the breakfast-room. Barton had come to realize that Lady Augusta had been right about his rudeness to his bride, and also right in saying that it was Amanda's responsibility to see to the smooth operation of his household. He would be forced, he supposed, to apologize to Amanda. Barton's mouth twisted in a wry grimace. How ironic that he should feel compelled to beg pardon of the woman who had trapped him into marriage!

Then had come that unfortunate conversation with Carolyn. Barton now bitterly regretted taking such a high-handed tone with his former mistress. It had served no purpose but to inflame Carolyn; she would be as good as her word, Barton thought, and never rest until she had revenged herself upon him and Amanda. Carolyn's instant intuition that he might not have married Amanda willingly had shaken Barton, and he shuddered to think of the scandal that would ensue if she found proof of her suspicions and publicized them.

And the interview with Dennison had been the perfect cap to a perfect morning, Barton thought bitterly. Loath as he had been to believe Augusta's assertions about the untrustworthiness of his butler, Barton could not but allow that the man had seemed utterly unrepentant. And Barton was sure the hint he had dropped about Chas's attentions to Amanda had had no other purpose than to cause trouble between him and his wife.

"Bart!" Chas Wendover's voice lifted Barton from his brown study. "When did you get back? Lord, but you're a sight for sore eyes." Chas dropped into the seat across from Barton and grinned cheerfully at his friend.

Barton nodded. "I returned to Town last night," he said.

Chas gave Barton a wary look. "I never expected you to stay in Herefordshire so long."

"I didn't—I was escorting my grandmother back to Town," Barton explained. "We travelled by easy stages."

"Lady A is back in London?" Chas exclaimed. "Famous! I haven't seen her for far too long. She's quite one of my favourite people, you know." His smile wavered, then died. "How...how did she like Amanda?"

"Why, they're well on their way to being bosom bows," Barton said sourly. "Amanda's with her at this very moment, gadding about the town."

Chas's expression cleared. "Wonderful!"

Barton stared at Chas. "*Et tu,* Chas?"

"I hope you won't dislike it too much, old chum, but I've grown very fond of Amanda while you've been gone," Chas said apologetically.

"So I've heard," Barton said. "Dennison made it his business to tell me that you had been 'most flattering' in your attentions to her."

"The devil you say!" Chas exclaimed. "What cheek!" He shook his head. "I can't think why you don't give him the sack, Bart."

"Because I have a peculiar aversion to running my household to suit you!" Barton snapped.

Chas was surprised and a little hurt. "My apologies," he said stiffly.

Barton groaned. "No, Chas, mine! I'm an insufferable clunch. You mustn't mind a word I say."

"Is...is everything well at home?" Chas asked carefully.

"Just perfect!" Barton said. "I've a wife I don't know, a grandmother who hasn't stopped stamping her cane in days and a butler whom, apparently, no one of my acquaintance can abide!"

Chas grinned sympathetically. "Bit of a coil, ain't it?"

"To say the very least," Barton agreed.

"Still, it could be worse," Chas said. Barton cocked an enquiring brow at him. "At least you're free of Carolyn!"

Barton groaned again. "Did I neglect to mention that Lady Travers called on Amanda this morning? When I taxed Carolyn with it, we had a terrible row. She asked me flat out if Amanda had trapped me into marriage, which I denied, of course, in my most top-lofty fashion. I thereby succeeded in enraging Caro even more. She stormed out vowing revenge.''

"Those green-eyed females," Chas said darkly. "Didn't I warn you?"

"It is a little late for warnings now," Barton retorted. "The question is, how am I to keep Carolyn from making a scandal the likes of which London has never seen?"

Chas was silent for a long moment, then said, "It appears to me that the only way to convince the ton that you married Amanda of your own free will is to show them. You know—squire Amanda about Town, do the pretty...make them think it was a love match."

"I fear that you credit me with more dramatic skill than I possess," Barton said. "How the devil can I convince anyone that I am in love with Amanda when I don't even know her?"

"Well, get to know her!" Chas said. "Truth to tell, Bart, it's what you should do in any event. Amanda's a sweet little thing. I do believe that you'll be agreeably surprised in her, if only you give her a chance. A little kindness would go a long way with her."

"That's what Grandmama told me, too, more or less," Barton admitted.

"There you have it, then!" Chas said. "There's no one more alive to all suits than Augusta."

"How can I be kind to the girl when I can scarcely bear to be in the same room with her?" Barton burst out. "Every time I look at Amanda, I am reminded of what a fool I was."

Chas opened his mouth to speak, then closed it. He wished that he might tell Barton Amanda's story, but he had promised to keep her secret and a gentleman did not break a promise, especially one made to a lady. "She's not what you think her, Bart, I'm sure of it," he said finally. "Do try, won't you? Try to make friends with Amanda and see if you do not come to agree with me."

Barton sighed, then shrugged. "Very well," he said. "In deference to you, and to Grandmama, I will try. But don't let your hopes soar too high, my friend. I cannot think it likely that Amanda and I will ever learn to be anything more than cordial strangers!"

AMANDA FROWNED and turned the bedsheet she was stitching a little more towards the light. She was curled up in a chair in the drawing-room, her feet tucked underneath her and a branch of working candles set near at hand. She applied herself to the sewing for several minutes, then caught a flash of movement out of the corner of her eye and looked up to find Barton watching her.

"Oh!" she said, and jumped up. "My...my lord! I did not hear you come in."

Barton bent to pick up the linen that had slipped from Amanda's lap. "How should you?" he said. "You were engrossed in your work. Doing a bit of fancy sewing?"

"No, I am repairing this sheet," Amanda said. "Mrs. Mandley was kind enough to show me through the house today, and I noticed these lovely old bedlinens that needed only a touch of repair to be perfectly usable.''

"There's no need for you to do the household sewing,'' Barton said. "The servants are here to see to such things.''

"Oh, but I wanted to do it,'' Amanda said. "And I promise you, my work is very good—I set a pretty stitch, if I do say so myself.'' She held the sheet out to Barton.

He took it clumsily. "Indeed, I cannot even discern your repairs,'' he said. "It is... very good of you to trouble yourself with it.'' Amanda coloured prettily.

She sat back down, and an uncomfortable silence fell between them.

"So!'' Barton said too heartily. "Have you been busy today?''

"Lady Augusta took me calling,'' Amanda said. "We visited four or five of her friends in all.''

Barton grimaced comically. "A devilish dull day, I have no doubt.''

Amanda smiled briefly. "It was not so very bad,'' she said. "Everyone was most... civil.''

Barton frowned. "Cut up stiff, did they?''

"No, no, no one would dare! Lady Augusta was at her most formidable,'' Amanda responded. "Lady Admore did ask me, in the most forward way imaginable, if I had known you for very long, but Lady Augusta soon made her wish that she had never spoken.''

"I'll wager she did.'' Barton grinned, genuinely amused. "I have no doubt that Grandmama rang a royal peal over the old harridan. I only wish that I had been there to hear it!''

"So did Lady Augusta," Amanda said drily. "She seemed a trifle put out with you for going abroad this afternoon—she had thought that you would accompany us on our calls."

"Lord save me from that," Barton said. "Did you suffer her wrath in my absence?"

"Lady Augusta was very kind," Amanda said quietly. "More so than I deserved, perhaps."

Barton stiffened; was Amanda finally admitting her fault?

"I did nothing wrong!" Amanda cried, stung by Barton's reaction. "But that does not matter, does it?" Amanda took a deep breath, then continued more moderately. "Lady Augusta has every reason, in her own mind, to think me the most irreclaimable of hoydens. Why then should she be so kind to me?"

"Because she is a lady, in every sense of the word," Barton said. "And because she has reason to remember your grandfather with great fondness."

"Of course," Amanda agreed.

Barton was startled by the wistfulness of her tone. To cover his surprise, he fumbled in his pocket and took out a small velvet box. "This is for you," he said awkwardly, and dropped it into Amanda's lap.

Amanda looked blank. "What is it?"

"Call it a bride gift," Barton said wryly. "And an apology—I was most uncivil this morning, and for that, I am truly sorry." When Amanda still hesitated, he added, "Go ahead, open it."

She lifted the lid and gasped. A ring lay nestled in the crimson velvet, a magnificent table-cut emerald surrounded by diamonds.

"My lord!" Amanda said faintly. "I cannot accept . . . that is to say, it would not be proper . . ."

"Nonsense," Barton said gruffly. "It is a tradition in our family to give one's bride a jewel. Would you have me fly in the face of tradition?"

Amanda hesitantly touched the emerald with one finger. "It is so beautiful!"

"It reminded me of a necklace that has been in the family for ages," Barton told her.

"It is quite the loveliest thing I have ever seen," Amanda said, with a simplicity that lent her words sincerity.

"Why don't you try it on?" Barton suggested.

Still Amanda hesitated. "If you are quite sure that you want me to have it . . . ?"

Barton took the box from her, removed the ring and slipped it onto her finger. "There," he said. "A perfect fit." He felt her fingers tremble in his own and frowned. "Amanda? What is it?"

She blushed hotly, for she could not tell Barton that it was his closeness that discomfited her! The warm touch of his hand and the pressure of his fingers reminded her of the feel of his body against hers in the carriage and made her pulses leap. "I—I—" she stammered.

"You mustn't be afraid of me, Amanda," Barton said softly. Looking into her eyes, he realized that they were exactly the colour of a rich Bordeaux. They glowed in the light of the work candles and seemed to invite a closer inspection. Almost without realizing it, Barton dropped to one knee beside Amanda's chair. "Are you?"

"Am I...am I what?" Amanda whispered. She did not move away as Barton came closer to her.

"Are you afraid of me?" Barton breathed. His gaze moved from her eyes to her lips, moist and slightly parted. He wondered what it would be like to kiss her and almost against his will moved still closer to his wife, bent his head and...

"A pretty picture!" Barton and Amanda looked up, Amanda's hand still lightly resting in Barton's, to find Lady Augusta watching them, one eyebrow raised. "Very affecting, to be sure," she said drily. She examined Amanda's ring and nodded approval. "A good notion, Barton, if a trifle past time," she said. "It would have been thought passing strange for your bride to wear no token of your regard!" She did not wait for her grandson to answer, but continued, "You'll be happy to know that Amanda did nicely today, Barton. She behaved very prettily. I had nothing to blush for in either her deportment or her manners." She favoured Amanda with a brisk nod. "Well done!"

Amanda blushed furiously. "You are...very, very kind, ma'am," she said faintly.

"Don't be missish, now, girl," Lady Augusta said sharply. "It don't become you."

"Amanda tells me that you saw Lady Admore," Barton said, his eyes bright with laughter. "How did you find her?"

Lady Augusta snorted. "The bird-witted fool! She actually dared to attempt a high tone with me, when I know to a day how old she is, and how old that young fiancé of hers thinks her!"

Amanda giggled suddenly, then pressed her hand to her mouth. "I am sorry," she said, trying without success to school her features into some semblance of gravity. "But it does explain your reference to mutton dressed as lamb...!"

Barton gave a great shout of laughter. "Grandmama, you devil!"

Lady Augusta smiled thinly. "That Admore woman shan't trifle again with me or mine, of that you may be quite sure." Lady Augusta settled herself into an armchair, waving Barton away as he stepped forward to help her. "Now," she said briskly, "I'd like to talk to you both about the ball."

Amanda looked blank. Barton said cautiously, "What ball?"

Lady Augusta fixed him with a steely stare. "The ball that you will host in one week's time."

Amanda drew in her breath as Barton said, "What? Now, really, Grandmama...it cannot be done!"

"Of course it can," Lady Augusta said. "In point of fact, I have already begun the invitations. You may help me with them, Amanda."

"But why the dev...why the rush?" Barton recovered himself hastily. "Surely there's no need for this infernal haste?"

"Would I put myself to so much trouble if I did not think it necessary?" Lady Augusta asked.

Barton frowned. "I thought you said your calls went well."

"I said that Amanda did well," Lady Augusta corrected him. "And so she did! But there is no denying that a deal of unpleasant talk is going the rounds. I propose to put a stop to it."

"But will anyone come?" Amanda asked. "With only a few days' notice..."

"Oh, they'll come," Lady Augusta said grimly. "Hoping for a scene, most of them, and all eyes and ears for gossip, but they'll come!"

"Do you really think this wise, Grandmama?" Barton asked doubtfully.

"I do," Lady Augusta said. "As much as I detest the thought of pandering to the impertinent, the sooner we allow the gossip-mongers to stare their fill, the sooner they'll leave us in peace. In short, my dears, lest we desire to spend the rest of the Season as the cynosure of all eyes, we had best face the ton and dare them to doubt us!"

VICOMTE DEVALME lifted a hand to hail Cecil Stratton, who was just entering the club known as the Cocoa Tree. "Well met, *mon vieux*," he said. "Will you share a glass of wine?" He pushed the decanter towards Cecil and snapped his fingers at the waiter for another glass. "You'll find it pleasing, I think."

Cecil permitted the waiter to fill his glass, then took a sip. "Very nice," he said. "A Bordeaux?"

"Hardly," DeValme drawled.

Cecil gave a sickly smile. "Truth to tell, I've no palate for wine," he admitted. "It all tastes the same to me!"

"Now why is it that I do not find that difficult to believe?" DeValme asked, the sarcasm in his voice all the more cutting for its undercurrent of amusement.

Cecil scowled. "I'm surprised that you have time to take a glass of wine with me," he said belligerently, "busy as you have been of late."

DeValme shrugged. "One wishes to see and hear, my friend," he said. "I visit, I listen, I hear all the *on dits* and the—what is the phrase?—ah yes, the 'crim. con.' stories. It was moderately rewarding." He took another sip of wine, and added, "Particularly at White's."

Cecil's scowl deepened. "You went to White's?" he said. "I can't think why—it's the flattest place in Town."

"One must visit White's when one is in London. It is *de rigueur*—one of the sights, in fact." DeValme chuckled deep in his throat. "Quite picturesque, in its way."

"How is it that you come to be a member?" Cecil challenged him. "I'm not, and I'm English!"

"It was *mon parrain*—my godfather, you understand," DeValme said. "He was English. He put my name up for membership when I was a mere sprig."

Cecil gave a crack of rude laughter. "Just as well that he did put you up when you were a lad," he said. "You'd never be allowed membership by those top-lofty snobs now, not with your reputation!"

DeValme stared at his companion; the colour drained out of Cecil's face, and he began to stammer an apology. DeValme continued staring until Cecil's words trailed to a halt. Then the *vicomte* went on speaking, as though Cecil had never interrupted him.

"Yes, my visit to White's was most enlightening," he said. "I saw Barton there."

"You did?" Cecil leaned forward in his seat. "Did you speak to him?"

"But of course," DeValme said. "I felt that I must make a leg to this gentleman whom our Amanda has wed, so I found some handy fool to introduce us." DeValme toyed with his quizzing glass. "His lordship was not pleased to see me, and he did not trouble to hide his distaste. Lord Barton did not approve!" DeValme's eyes were hooded. "Though my family was noble when his forefathers were still rolling about in the muck, he dared to judge me. I found it most amusing." DeValme did not look amused.

Cecil made a moue of distaste. "Barton can be a dashed ugly customer when he climbs onto his high horse," he said, "as I have reason to know."

"You misunderstand," DeValme said. "Barton was the model of politeness—offensively so, in fact. It fell to his friend Mr. Wendover to growl at me."

"That young jackanapes is a deal too forward with his opinions," Cecil said. "He was positively surly when I encountered him at Barton's."

"It appears that he has appointed himself Amanda's chevalier," DeValme said. "When I merely mentioned her name, this Wendover broke in and was uncivil in the extreme."

"Do tell," Cecil said, his eyes bright with malice. "Did you call him out?"

"Of course not," DeValme said. "He is no more than *un moucheron*—a gnat, buzzing about. Irritating, mayhap, and someday one may choose to squash him, but not, you understand, of any importance. No, it is Barton who interests me—he is arrogant, that one!

I feel that I must school him. But how best to accomplish his education?'' DeValme regarded his wine-glass absently. ''To kill him would be too easy. Of a certainty, it must be his pride that is broken.''

''It may prove to be a difficult task, that,'' Cecil said. ''Barton is up to every rig in Town.''

''True,'' DeValme agreed. ''But he seems quite determined to play into my hands. Already he has set his foot on the path to destruction. As I told you, I have been looking and listening. And what I hear, *mon vieux,* is that there is something strange about this sudden marriage of Barton's. No one questions it aloud—the hypocritical English shrink from confrontation. But they watch...and wonder.'' DeValme was lost in contemplation for a moment. ''Who is Carolyn Travers?'' he asked finally.

Cecil blinked. ''Barton's mistress,'' he said. ''Though it is not generally known, la Travers is definitely his *chère amie.* Or *was*—rumour has it that Barton gave her her *congé* shortly before his recent trip to France.''

''Did he now?'' DeValme smiled. ''Tell me about this Carolyn.''

''A beauty, of course,'' Cecil said. ''Black hair, green eyes, skin like the richest cream...!'' Cecil seemed lost in a pleasant reverie. ''Devil of a temper, though,'' he continued after a moment. ''One of those hotheaded females who are capable of any fit or start when they're in a passion.''

''Ah, Barton,'' DeValme said softly, ''how heedlessly you rush to your fate!''

"What on earth do you mean?" Cecil demanded irritably.

"It simply occurs to me," DeValme said, "that a spurned woman is a powerful enemy. And the enemy of my enemy is my friend, is that not so?"

"I'd wager that she's angry enough with Barton to be ripe for any lark," Cecil allowed. "I always thought that Carolyn fancied herself as Lady Barton."

"Did she? Better and better! Do you know her?"

Cecil shrugged. "Not to say *know*—we have met."

"Very good," DeValme said briskly. "You may introduce me to her, then. She shall be my ally! And will it not be delicious? The proud Lord Barton, humbled by a man he loathes and by his former mistress."

"I don't see how you'll manage it," Cecil said doubtfully. "Mean to say, Barton's not some green lad ripe for the plucking. If you won't call him out..."

"You underestimate my powers, *mon ami*," DeValme said. "Finesse will win the day, and cunning." He lazily spun his quizzing glass on its cord. "Never doubt that I shall craft a fate for Barton—and his lady!—that will make them wish that they had never thought to mock me."

CHAPTER EIGHT

AMANDA'S MAID gave one final pat to Amanda's coiffure and stepped back. "Oh, my lady," she breathed. "You do look a treat!"

Amanda shyly regarded her reflection in the mirror. She had chosen a simply styled cream-coloured satin gown for the ball; her maid had gathered her hair high on her head, in a golden fillet, and let it tumble down her back in a cascade of auburn curls. Around her neck hung a magnificent collar of heavy chased gold and large table-cut emeralds.

Lady Augusta, seated in a corner of Amanda's bedchamber, smiled her approval. "You look charmingly, my dear," she said warmly. "And the necklace is perfect—I'm glad that Barton thought to have the family jewels taken out of the vault for you." She waved Amanda's maid out of the room.

"It was very kind in him to think of it," Amanda said. "Though it seems very strange to me to be wearing anything so grand!"

"Don't be ridiculous," Lady Augusta said in the sharp way which Amanda had come to realize denoted affection. "You have every right in the world to wear any of that jewellery. In fact, you're obliged to! Barton is the head of the family, and you are his wife.

They're yours, until you have a son to pass them on to."

Amanda blushed hotly and Lady Augusta held out a hand to her. "You mustn't mind me, girl. I tend to speak my mind when I should hold my tongue."

The past week had been a time of frenzied activity for Lady Augusta and Amanda. The effort required to mount a ball in just seven days was enormous; the two woman had, by necessity, spent almost every waking hour together, planning, shopping, overseeing and ordering. In that time, they had grown—much to their mutual surprise—to greatly enjoy each other's company.

"Now, you mustn't be thrown off your stride by this evening's event," Lady Augusta said. "I wish I could tell you that they won't stare—but they will! You must not let such impertinence trouble you, though. You are a Barton, and Bartons endure. Simply lift your head high and carry on."

"I'll do my best," Amanda promised. She pressed both hands hard against her middle. "I am a trifle nervous, though, I must allow!"

"Nerves," Lady Augusta said acerbically, "are for those who need to make themselves interesting. Do not, pray, ally yourself with such an insipid group!"

Amanda was startled into silence by Lady Augusta's vehemence. The dowager continued, "For whatever it is worth, my dear, you need not worry that I shall be looking to find fault with you. I've watched you, and listened to you, and...well, you are the general all over again. I can say no higher than that!" Lady Augusta watched Amanda shrewdly. "What freakish circumstances brought you on board ship that night I do not wish to know—you had much better explain them to your husband. But I do believe with all my heart that you were not there to trap my grandson, and I know that this marriage was as distasteful to you as it was to Barton. That you have done your best with a bad situation is greatly appreciated, by me, if no one else."

The old woman chuckled. "The difference you've made in the running of this household is quite shocking.... Did you know that my morning's water today was actually hot? That is an unprecedented occurrence, I promise you! You may be sorry for it, though, in the end. You've made the place so comfortable that I may wish to visit much more often."

Amanda squeezed Lady Augusta's hand warmly. "You are welcome to stay forever," she said. "And Barton would be thrilled if you would remain here with us—he loves you very much, you know."

"As I do him," Lady Augusta said. "That's why I shall take it upon myself to say one more thing, though it's none of my concern. But I promise you, I'll meddle this once and then never again." She met Amanda's eyes soberly. "Barton is a good man, Amanda. You've not seen him at his best. Pray don't judge him too harshly! Only give him a little time, and he'll do better."

Amanda smiled, a little sadly. "He has not been so very bad, truly. Since the night he gave me my ring—" she touched it affectionately "—he has been unfailingly courteous."

"But . . . ?" Augusta prompted her.

"But if you cherish the hope that some warmer relationship may develop between us, you deceive yourself, ma'am. I can see it in Barton's eyes. He will never be able to forget, or forgive, the manner of our marriage."

Lady Augusta regarded the girl keenly. "And what of you, child? Can you forget? Can you forgive?"

"It does not matter," Amanda said, and turned away from Lady Augusta.

"Never mind, then," Lady Augusta said, not displeased by what she had read in Amanda's face. "I'll not pursue the matter if it distresses you. But remember this, my dear—no matter what, I shall stand your friend." The old woman's eyes took on a decided twinkle. "And I am, I promise you, as formidable a friend as I am an enemy!"

THE CROWD of guests moved slowly up the stairs that led to the ballroom in a living river of colour. Jewels flashed and a myriad of decorated fans fluttered as their owners prepared to meet the new Lady Barton. Everywhere could be heard the buzz of excited conversation.

This evening's entertainment had broken over the ton like a storm. The invitations, sent out such a short time beforehand, had provoked speculation of the most intriguing kind and had quickly become the most sought after items in London. Everyone who was anyone had been asked, and there was no one invited who did not plan to attend. Modistes all over Town had been besieged; ladies in a frenzy to be *au courant* had threatened, cajoled and bribed their dressmakers to secure promises of suitable raiment.

The gentlemen of the ton had been almost as curious as their ladies. They had sat in their clubs, wondering what the devil Barton was about, and why a man who was known to detest entertaining should suddenly decide to host a ball. One man, who had suggested that Barton merely wished to introduce his bride to Society, was universally ignored, for if that were Barton's only aim, why such indecent haste in mounting the whole affair? The ton sensed a mystery, and there was nothing they enjoyed more. So they flocked to the ball, and thus fulfilled Lady Augusta's cynical predictions.

The dowager took advantage of a gap in the crowd of arrivals to squeeze Amanda's hand. "You're doing wonderfully well, child," Lady Augusta said. "Isn't she, Barton?"

Barton smiled down at his wife. "She is," he replied with more warmth than Amanda had ever heard in his voice. In truth, Barton was pleased and surprised by how well the evening was going. Though it was, he reminded himself, early times yet!

From the first, Barton had been deeply troubled by Lady Augusta's insistence on holding the ball; he had thought Amanda too unknown a quantity to risk exposing her to Society en masse. The girl had shown herself to be moderately well-mannered, it was true, but Barton had been uncertain how she would react to the staring eyes and politely worded interrogations of the ton. But from the moment Lady Augusta and Amanda had appeared to take their places beside

Barton at the head of the stairs, nothing had gone quite as he had expected.

The sight of Amanda dressed in her finery had startled Barton almost into speechlessness. Though he had acknowledged to himself that his bride was a pretty girl, he had not been prepared for the vision standing at Lady Augusta's side. Her cheeks glowing in a faint blush, her eyes sparkling and her lips lifted in a shy smile, Amanda was a veritable beauty. And Barton was not alone in realizing that fact, he soon saw. The appreciative looks of more than one gentleman paid tribute to Amanda's loveliness.

Nor had his wife's behaviour been found wanting. Amanda's manner was neither coming nor backward; her shy friendliness struck just the right note with both ladies and gentleman.

"You are to be congratulated, Amanda," Barton said lightly. "Even the haughty Countess Lieven unbent enough to favour you with a smile."

"And the promise of a voucher to Almack's," Lady Augusta added smugly.

Barton laughed. "A coup, indeed!" he said, and they turned back to their guests.

As the ladies and gentlemen of the haut ton continued to stream up the stairs, Amanda felt as though she had fallen into a dream. How could she ever have imagined, during that nightmare flight from De-Valme's château, that she would end up here, the new Lady Barton, greeting her fashionable guests by her husband's side?

She stole a look at Barton. He was handsome, she was bound to admit, and so very elegant! Her untutored eye could not name the tailor who had cut her husband's clothes, but that they had come from the hand of a master was evident. The evening coat and knee breeches fit him without a wrinkle; his snowy-white neckcloth was arranged with tasteful artistry, a large emerald nestled in its folds. Though scores of gentleman had taken her hand and smiled at her this night, Amanda could not recall one who looked more distinguished than her husband. Just at that moment, Barton caught her eyes on him and smiled. Amanda thought with a start that she was actually proud to be the lady on his arm! Dazedly, she wondered if perhaps—just perhaps—this marriage might prove not to have been such a great mistake, after all?

Dennison moved to Lord Barton's side and spoke quietly into his ear. Barton scowled and leaned towards Augusta. "There is some difficulty in the kitchens," he said softly. "I'll have to go and see what's amiss."

Amanda slid the ribbon of her fan over her wrist and took her skirts in hand. "I shall see to it, my lord," she said briskly. "It is more fitting that..."

Barton lightly touched Amanda's shoulder, and the feel of his palm against her bare shoulder made Amanda start. Barton's eyes widened, then he frowned. After a moment, he said gruffly, "There's no need for you to disturb yourself, my dea...Amanda. I'll go down myself. I've a few choice words to say to the genius who rules my ovens!" He moved off, smiling and bowing as he made his way through the crowd.

From her position behind one of the pillars flanking the stairs, Carolyn Travers smiled. *A guinea well spent!* she thought complacently, and moved out of her hiding place.

Lady Augusta had turned away for a moment to speak to an old friend; she did not see Carolyn run lightly up the stairs and stop in front of Amanda.

"Good evening, my dear Lady Barton!" Carolyn glittered in green satin that exactly matched her eyes and the emerald necklace that hung round her white throat. "How good of you to have me—or is it Barton I must thank for my invitation?" In fact, Carolyn had received no card of invitation, but she was sure that neither Barton nor Lady Augusta, and certainly not Amanda, would dare to make a scene by having her ejected. "Such a picture you look," Carolyn went on. "So simple and sweet!" She noticed the antique necklace that Amanda wore, and laughed throatily. "How ridiculously fond of emeralds Barton is," she remarked, touching the jewels that hung around her own throat.

"Lady Travers," Lady Augusta said coldly, having heard Carolyn's last words.

"Good evening, Lady Augusta," Carolyn said. "How do you do this evening?" Her bold stare challenged the elderly woman.

Lady Augusta's jaw clenched as she struggled with herself. "I am very well, Lady Travers," she said finally. "You may count yourself lucky indeed if you do so well!" Carolyn inclined her head mockingly and moved into the ballroom.

Amanda pressed a hand weakly to her burning cheeks. As the flood of arrivals had finally started to lessen, Lady Augusta was able to draw Amanda into a convenient alcove.

"That infamous woman," she fumed. "How dare she show her face here?"

"She said...she said that she was invited," Amanda said. "She told me that Barton..."

"Nonsense," Lady Augusta said flatly. "Barton has too much sense to have invited that brazen hussy tonight of all nights."

Amanda looked away. Was it likely, she thought bleakly, that Barton would have told his grandmother that he had invited his mistress to their ball?

Lady Augusta squeezed Amanda's hands. "We shan't let it spoil our evening, though, shall we? Let's away into the ballroom. It is past time that you started to enjoy yourself, child!" She led Amanda out of the recess.

"If it's enjoyment you're looking for, then I'm your man." Chas Wendover approached them with his characteristic good humour. "I bid you good evening, Amanda," he said, bowing over her hand. "You look quite lovely, my dear." He turned to Lady Augusta. "My lady!" He clasped a hand theatrically to his heart. "A ravishing creature, in truth. When will you be mine and end this sweet torment?"

Lady Augusta rapped Chas sharply on the wrist with her fan; he was a prime favourite of hers. "Go along with you, rogue," she said. "I won't have you spouting such fustian to me, and I old enough to be your grandmama!"

"'Age cannot wither her, nor custom stale, her infinite variety....'" Chas grinned cheekily at Augusta.

"Is my benighted friend troubling you, ladies?" Barton asked as he rejoined them. "If so, I'll have him hurled from the ramparts." He waved an arm extravagantly.

"Not before I've waltzed with Lady Augusta, you won't," Chas said. "You could not be cruel enough to deny a doomed man his last request, could you, my lady?"

"There's no need for Barton to hurl you from anything, Chas," Lady Augusta commented drily. "I'm quite convinced that you'll end your days on the gallows!" She tucked her arm into his. "If you've no fear of appearing ridiculous by waltzing with such a dried-up old thing as I, then so be it!"

Barton held out his arm to Amanda. "Shall we go?"

"Very well, my lord," Amanda said in a colourless voice, and laid her hand on Barton's arm.

Barton frowned. "Is something amiss?" Amanda did not answer, and he added sharply, "What has happened to overset you?"

"Come along, children," Chas said cheerfully. "Time to face the lions! 'We who are about to die...'"

Lady Augusta snorted. "You may see yourself as a martyr, young man, but I most assuredly do not. Let them, rather, beware of me!"

Barton and Amanda stepped through the double doors first, with Chas and Lady Augusta just behind them. The ballroom was a spacious chamber, with lofty ceilings and crystal chandeliers that gleamed like captive stars. On a raised platform at one end of the room an orchestra was playing a quiet Brahms air, as the dancing had not yet begun. A large card room that opened off the other side of the room offered tables, cards and all else necessary to keep those guests not interested in dancing happily occupied.

All eyes turned to the entrance as Barton and Amanda came in. Amanda coloured prettily, but Barton could feel her trembling. For a moment, he covered her hand with his, then he signalled to the orchestra leader, and the musicians struck up a waltz.

"May I have this dance, Lady Barton?" he asked with a smile.

For a moment it looked as though Amanda would refuse her husband. Then she lifted her head proudly. "Yes," she said.

Barton put his arm around her, and they swept out onto the floor. For several moments, no one joined them and Amanda felt, not without some justification, as though every pair of eyes in the room were fixed on them. Then other couples began to dance, and it was all she could do not to heave a sigh of relief.

"There, now," Barton said. "That was not so bad, was it?"

"Not for you, perhaps," Amanda returned. "But then, they are your friends, are they not?"

"Good God, no!" Barton exclaimed. "Of the four hundred guests we invited, perhaps twenty or so are what I should call friends. The rest? Acquaintances, some of them, and relations, and a throng of gossips who are, alas, too well-born for us to snub."

"They, at least, must be enjoying themselves," Amanda said. "There is much for them to discuss, after all."

"But there will be less tomorrow," Barton said seriously. "If we can make them believe that we are happy together, the talk will die down, I promise you."

"How, precisely, are we to do that when Carolyn Travers is here to make sure that the ton knows how far from contentment we are?" Amanda asked bitterly.

Barton frowned. "Caro is here?"

"You need not pretend ignorance, my lord," Amanda said. "Lady Travers seemed most eager to thank you for her card of invitation. Indeed, it was kind in you to think of her. I vow, neither Lady Augusta nor I ever considered asking her."

Amanda's words stung him. "Are you really preaching to me of propriety?" Barton asked coldly. "I should not think that even you would have such impertinence."

"At least I had the common sense not to do that which would be bound to occasion even more talk," Amanda retorted. "I realize that I am, in truth, no wife to you, but to invite your mistress? I thought that the purpose of this evening's entertainment was to squelch gossip, not to cause it."

Lady Augusta, watching Barton and Amanda from afar, sighed and shook her head. Chas, who was standing just behind her, asked softly, "They're quarrelling, aren't they?"

"Drat their stubbornness!" Lady Augusta said. "They would be perfect for each other if only they'd forget their pride and get on with it!" She glanced at Chas. "I shouldn't be saying such things to you, I suppose, but I count you as part of the family, boy."

Chas tucked her arm through his companionably. "Thank you!" he said. "And if it's any comfort to you, I think you're absolutely right...about Bart and Amanda, that is. What can we do?"

"Nothing, more's the pity," Lady Augusta said gruffly. "They must settle it themselves. Interference invariably does more harm than good."

Chas looked away from Lady Augusta and stiffened. "What," he asked incredulously, "is Cecil Stratton doing here?"

"I invited him," Lady Augusta said. "And you needn't look so amazed, sir! As little as we may like it, he is Amanda's uncle. It would have looked very peculiar indeed had we not asked him to attend."

"Good Lord," Chas said faintly, still looking over his companion's shoulder. "He's brought DeValme with him!" Chas made as if to move past Lady Augusta. "We shall see about this," he said grimly. "I'll have that bounder out before—"

Lady Augusta laid a restraining hand on Chas's shoulder. "Hold!" she said. "Much as I dislike to say it, we shall have to endure DeValme's presence."

"You can't mean it!" Chas protested.

"We dare not make a scene—it would be the worst thing possible for poor Amanda," Lady Augusta pointed out. "It is in her best interests, and Barton's, that we try to ignore DeValme's presence."

"We may be able to," Chas said, "but Barton will not. Look!"

The waltz had ended, and Barton and Amanda were moving off the floor. As they stepped out of the crowd of dancers, Cecil and DeValme joined them.

"Good evening, Amanda," Cecil said, beaming cheerfully. "Barton—a wonderful party! It will be deemed that pinnacle of social praise, a sad crush, I have no doubt." He waved a hand at DeValme. "You remember the *vicomte,* my lord?"

Barton drew himself up stiffly. "Indeed," he said distantly. DeValme inclined his head.

"And of course I need not introduce DeValme to you, Amanda," Cecil said roguishly. "I do not scruple to tell you, my lord, that the *vicomte* greatly admires my niece."

Barton looked at Amanda in disbelief as DeValme bowed over her hand.

"Good evening, Lady Barton," DeValme said. "How lovely you are!" He held her hand for a moment longer than was strictly necessary. "More lovely than ever, in fact."

Amanda pulled her hand free. "You flatter me dreadfully, I fear," she said coldly. "There are many ladies here this evening who are far more beautiful than I."

"Not so," DeValme said. He looked boldly at Barton. "Would you not agree with me, my lord?"

Barton took a firm grip on Amanda's arm. "I must bow to your superior knowledge of feminine pulchritude," he said, and began to move away. "You will excuse us . . . ?"

DeValme bowed again. "Of course," he said gracefully. "Would you permit me to call on you, my lady?"

"I think not," Barton said flatly.

Despite her anger at Barton, Amanda was happy, in this instance, to let him speak for her. "Good evening, gentlemen."

Cecil and DeValme watched Lord and Lady Barton move away. DeValme chuckled softly.

"You're damned happy for a man who's just been thoroughly snubbed," Cecil said, his voice full of sly amusement. "I shouldn't have thought that you'd endure such impertinence."

"I endure…temporarily," DeValme said, his good humour not one whit diminished. "Never doubt that I shall have my moment." He stared after Barton, and his smile widened. "And now, if you please, I should greatly like to meet Lady Travers!"

CHAPTER NINE

AMANDA LEFT the heavy doors ajar and stepped into the empty ballroom. The servants had done their tasks well: the room was clean and polished, the chandeliers once more swathed in their linen covers and the gilt chairs stacked neatly along the walls. All the flowers had long since been removed, but Amanda fancied that she could still detect a lingering hint of their sweetness in the air.

She shivered suddenly, and moved to close the French doors at the end of the room. However, when she reached them, she only stood, hands on the latches, staring out at the terrace. How peaceful it looked, she thought, and could barely contain a tart laugh.

When Barton had dragged her away from Cecil and DeValme the night before, he had brought her outside to the terrace.

"Do not think to trifle with me, Amanda," he had said tightly. "I shan't tolerate it!" He had scowled, and Amanda had seen the muscle twitch in his jaw.

She had pretended ignorance. "I have no idea what you are talking about," she had said. "And whatever it is, I do not wish to discuss it here, my lord—it is far too chilly."

"You will find yourself very much colder if you continue to provoke me," Barton had warned her. "I will not allow you to encourage that rake DeValme."

"I did not encourage him!" Amanda had said hotly.

"To be seen speaking to such a one is more than enough to make you the talk of the Town," Barton told her.

"Our guests will be far too busy discussing the appearance of your *chère amie* here this evening to bother themselves with me!"

She had had the satisfaction of seeing Barton flush. "Lady Travers is not my *chère amie!*"

"You may wish to tell her that," Amanda had answered sweetly. "She appears to believe otherwise."

"I warned you before we married that I would not suffer your hoydenish ways," Barton had said harshly. "And I do not intend to, Amanda. You would do well to recall what you owe to me, and to my name."

"What I *owe* to you?" Amanda had been flushed with rage. "I owe you nothing—nothing! And I will not be ruled by you! I will behave as I see fit. And if you do not like it, well! All the worse for you, my lord."

"Did I think that you meant that..."

"Why should you doubt it?" Amanda had taunted him, too angry to care about anything but hurting Barton as he had hurt her. "If I did not cavil at luring you into marriage, why should any lesser sin cause me so much as a moment's hesitation?"

Barton had stared at her for a long moment, his eyes narrowed. "To think," he had said bitterly, "that I'd almost begun to wonder if I had misjudged you! It only demonstrates once again, madam, that first impressions are invariably correct.'' Without another word he had turned on his heel and left. For the rest of the evening, Amanda had barely seen him.

She sighed tiredly now, and closed the French doors. Though the ball had not ended until very late, Amanda had been unable to sleep. She had tossed and turned and told herself that her husband had deserved everything that she'd said and done, but to no avail. Amanda felt slightly sick when she thought of what had passed between them, of how she had taunted her husband by saying that she had deliberately trapped him. There was no avoiding it; she had behaved badly, very badly. Blind with anger over Carolyn's presence last night, she had done everything possible to confirm Barton's bad opinion of her.

''Why so pensive, fair one?''

Amanda whirled about with a gasp. The Vicomte DeValme stood by the doors that led into the room, a slim, elegant figure dressed all in black. He cocked a brow at Amanda. ''My apologies,'' he said. ''I had not thought to terrify you!''

''What are you doing here?'' she asked bluntly. ''And why did Dennison not announce you?''

''The fault is mine, dear lady,'' DeValme told her. ''I managed to persuade your butler to allow me to announce myself.'' He did not mention that a handsome *douceur* had induced Dennison to grant his request. ''And as to why I'm here…I wished to see you, Amanda,'' he said.

"Did you?" Amanda lifted her head proudly. "I can't imagine why. We have nothing to say to each other, my lord."

"I could not help but notice that Lord Barton appeared a trifle put out when I arrived last evening," DeValme said calmly, ignoring Amanda's rudeness. "And when Cecil told him that you and I were acquainted, he appeared . . . well, I can only say that I'm sorry. I shouldn't have come last night if I had known that my lord would dislike it, or that he might blame you."

Amanda's sceptical expression spoke volumes. "Have I really given you so much reason to regard me with suspicion, child?" he continued. "I had thought that you were made tolerably comfortable when you were a guest at my château."

"Not a guest, my lord, but a prisoner," Amanda said.

"If that is so, it was not my doing," the *vicomte* pointed out. "As I recall, it was Cecil who brought you to France, not I."

"He brought me to be your bride," Amanda said baldly. "A position to which, I must assure you, I did not aspire!"

"Because of my infamous reputation, no doubt," DeValme observed. "Perhaps that is why you fled my home so precipitately?" He shook his head. "I pity you, my dear. After hearing the sort of lurid lies that people tell of me, you doubtless feared to be gagged and bound and dragged to the altar. I must tell you that I had no such plan—indeed, did I ever so much as mention the subject of marriage to you?"

"No," Amanda allowed, "but Cecil . . ."

"Cecil," DeValme said gently, "is both morally and intellectually wanting—surely you cannot disagree with me on that point? I realize that he is of your family, but every family has its scoundrel."

Amanda was frankly puzzled. "But are not you yourself a scoundrel, my lord?" she asked forthrightly. "Your reputation is so horrible!"

"Ah, rumour," DeValme remarked. "It has a way of taking on a life of its own! What begins as an amusing story becomes something very different—it is told and retold, exaggerated and embellished until it is something to frighten children with, a tale horrifying and sinister."

"Are you saying that all the stories about you are false?" Amanda asked, frankly incredulous. "Could hearsay stray so far from the truth?"

"Ah, I see that you hold to the theory of no smoke without fire," DeValme said calmly. "For myself, I can only say that I have sometimes been veritably blinded by smoke, with precious little fire to show for it!"

Amanda considered his words. After all, was it not the fear of gossip that had compelled her into this farce of a marriage? And further, if she and Barton had not wed, might the stories being told about them be as shocking as the tales of DeValme's supposed exploits?

"Ultimately, of course, you are asking me if I am . . . a sinner, shall we say?" DeValme shrugged gracefully. "I am," he admitted. "But tell me, child—what gentleman is not?" The shaft hit home; he saw

Amanda wince, her thoughts clearly turning to Barton and Carolyn, as he had intended they should. "There may exist that pure—and rare!—man who has never tasted the fruits of bachelorhood. If so, I have never met him. Have you?"

LORD BARTON SLAPPED his gloves against his palm impatiently, and consulted his pocket watch once more. He had not removed his many-caped driving cloak, and as a result, he had become overly warm, and even more irritated than he had been when first he arrived.

"*Chéri!*" Carolyn Travers swept into the drawing-room, wrapped in a velvet robe with long, trailing sleeves. "Have I kept you waiting, poor man?"

"As I was announced quite twenty minutes ago, you most certainly have!" Barton barked.

"And you are very cross, aren't you?" Carolyn smiled. "But you cannot blame me, love. You know how we ladies hate to be rushed, so you really should have taken off your things and made yourself comfortable." She curled up on a divan and patted the seat beside her. "Come, join me!"

"Thank you, no," Barton said. "What I have to say to you will take but a moment."

Carolyn's smile grew a shade more broad. "How very thrilling that sounds, to be sure."

"Why did you come to the ball last evening, Carolyn?" Barton was clearly attempting to keep a tight rein on his temper. "You must have noticed that you received no card of invitation."

"Do you know, I did notice that," Carolyn said thoughtfully. "A terrible oversight, to be sure. I can't imagine how it came about, can you?"

Barton took a deep breath. "I have no wish to pull caps with you, Caro, but this must stop. Can you not see that you are making both of us look the fool? And all out of some petty desire to hurt Amanda—that is why you came to the ball, isn't it? To tease my wife?"

"Oh, no, Bart, you misunderstand!" Carolyn cried. "I wished only to infuriate *you*, of course." She rose, and drifted towards him. "You were very cruel to me when last we met—did I not warn you that you should be sorry for it?" Carolyn stood very close to Barton. "You were terribly naughty, but now you have been spanked. I am willing to forget the whole matter, and I think that you are, too." Her heavy perfume filled Barton's nose; she gave a little laugh. "You cannot pretend that you are happy with that milk-and-water miss you've married. Everyone at the ball last night saw how very little to your taste she is."

Carolyn's words confirmed Barton's worst fears. The ball, which had been planned with the sole object of squelching gossip, had given the ton even more to talk about. Thanks, he thought bitterly, to his own stupidity! He had been so angry with Amanda when he left her on the terrace that he had taken himself off to the card room, there to play piquet with a few of his particular friends. He had barely seen his wife for the rest of the evening. However outrageously Amanda might have spoken to him, he had reacted in the worst possible way. Why was it that this girl should be able to so enrage him?

Lady Augusta had lost no time in pointing out the error of his ways to Barton. As soon as the last guest had departed, she had pulled her grandson into the library and rung a peal over his head. She had used the most intemperate of language to describe Barton's manners, his judgement and his sensitivity. When he had protested that Amanda's behaviour had been intolerable, Lady Augusta had retorted that the girl had been offered the most irresistible of provocations. After hearing the story of what had passed between Amanda and Carolyn upon Carolyn's arrival at the ball, Barton had been bound to own that his bride had had some excuse for her bad temper.

"Don't deny it, love...you miss me." Carolyn ran a finger lightly along the line of Barton's jaw. "I can feel it when I'm close to you."

"That proves only that your intuition is as faulty as your manners," Barton said coldly.

Carolyn was unfazed. "Is it? Somehow, I don't think so! If I were to do this—" she slipped her arms round Barton's neck and pressed close to him "—what do you suppose would happen?"

"Nothing." Barton removed Carolyn's arms and stepped back. "Nothing would happen now, Caro, nor ever will. I thought that I had made it quite clear to you that our association was at an end."

Carolyn's eyes narrowed, but she kept the smile firmly fixed on her face. "How unkind you are," she remarked. "You must be very angry, indeed! Shall I apologize, *chéri?* Will that make you regard me with a little more kindness?"

"I desire no apology from you—only your promise that you will keep your distance from both myself and my wife."

Carolyn attempted an airy tone. "You should not speak to me so, Bart. When you are so rough with me, it makes me very angry. And when I am angry—" she shrugged "—there is no telling what may happen!"

"Do not threaten me," Barton said flatly. "I'll tolerate only so much from you, Caro, and so I warn you."

Carolyn was fast losing what tenuous control she had over her temper. "Do not take such a high and mighty tone with me, if you please. I shall not be treated as though I were some dreadful *demi-mondaine!*"

Barton kept his expression carefully impassive, but what she saw in his eyes made Carolyn's fair skin redden in an unbecoming flush.

"You are become very strait-laced of a sudden, Barton," she hissed. "Do you plan to play the moralist for the ton? Shall you parade your bride and pretend to be a plaster saint? I might very easily put paid to that notion—I could tell the ton a pretty tale if I chose to!"

"Before you do, ask yourself this question: who would be most hurt by the story? Oh, I would be embarrassed, I don't deny it. And it might make Amanda somewhat uncomfortable, but since all sympathy would be with her, it would not be so very bad. But what of you, Caro? You would be scorned! People would say that you were no better than you should be, and turn their shoulders to you. Is that really what you want? To destroy your position in the ton and make an enemy of me, all for the fleeting satisfaction of causing Amanda and me some short-lived discomfort?''

"It would be well worth it, I vow, only to see that smug expression wiped from your face!" Carolyn retorted. "Do you really think that I shall allow you and that wife of yours to humiliate me? I will not. Be warned, Barton!''

Barton pulled on his gloves and moved towards the door. "It is, of course, your decision to make," he said with as much disinterest as he could feign. "But think well on it, Caro—think well indeed!''

A delicate Meissen vase shattered against the door as Barton closed it behind him. Carolyn looked wildly about her for something else to throw; when nothing presented itself, she began to stride up and down the length of the room, muttering to herself. "Insufferable prig! How could he speak to me so? It's that wife of his, I'll wager—she's put him up to this. Does she really think herself so much better than I? Does little Miss Butter-wouldn't-melt-in-her mouth believe that she can just snap her fingers and I will disappear? She is bound for a rude awakening, then, for if it is the last thing I do, I'll—''

What Carolyn would do was destined to remain unspoken, for at that moment the door opened and her maid entered. "Lady Travers," she began, "there's a Vicomte DeValme..."

DeValme stepped into the room on Mavis's heels. "My dear Lady Travers," he said smoothly. "How do you do?" He crossed the room to bow over her hand. "You must forgive me for taking advantage of our brief introduction last evening, but I could not resist the impulse to call. Say that you forgive me?''

Despite her upset, Carolyn preened. ''Of course, my lord,'' she said. ''Do, pray, make yourself comfortable.''

''I feared that I might have chosen a poor time to visit,'' DeValme said as he settled himself gracefully into an armchair. ''I saw Lord Barton leaving as my carriage pulled up, and I must tell you, he looked exceedingly wroth!''

''I am sure you are mistaken,'' Carolyn said, affecting an airy unconcern. ''He was perfectly calm when he left me.''

''I must beg leave to differ with you, my dear. I vow, his expression quite took me aback. He appeared to be in a powerful temper.''

Carolyn's colour rose, but she said only ''Barton and I are...old friends. We speak to each other with a great deal of freedom.''

''Indeed?'' DeValme said. ''Your generosity of spirit is remarkable.''

Carolyn's perfect brow wrinkled in a frown. ''I beg your pardon?''

''That you should still call Barton friend does you great credit,'' DeValme drawled. ''When one considers what is being said...''

''What do you mean? What is being said?''

DeValme shrugged gracefully. ''*Tout le monde* is abuzz with the story of how Barton has thrown you over. Everyone is gleaning a great deal of amusement from the tale, I fear.''

''What?'' Carolyn drew in her breath.

"It is most unfortunate, but really, not to be wondered at—such a delicious bit of gossip is quite irresistible." DeValme recrossed his legs. "The ton will have it that Barton simply tired of you. They intimate that you should have had the good sense to withdraw from his life on your own, before his lordship could grow weary of your charms. For myself, I believe that there is a bit more to it than that! I suspect that the new Lady Barton may have had a hand in your dismissal."

"I fail to see," Carolyn said through bloodless lips, "what possible concern this is of yours, my lord."

"Simply put, I cannot bear to see a beautiful woman made to look the fool," DeValme told her. "And I have my own reasons for disliking Lord and Lady Barton, and for wishing to be . . . how shall I put it . . . revenged upon them, I suppose you might say. I had thought that we two might be able to be of use to each other in this matter, but, if you still call Barton friend . . ." He shrugged again.

Carolyn sat, rigid with shock. They were amused, were they? And Barton and that chit he'd married were no doubt laughing loudest of all. Well, they would see how true the old adage was about he who laughs last! She eyed DeValme for a long moment, then leaned forward in her seat. "Tell me," she said simply, "how I can help?"

CHAPTER TEN

CHAS WENDOVER STARED gloomily down into his cup. He had come into the St. James's coffee-house looking for Barton; it was his fourth stop on a morning-long search for his friend, a search that had, so far, proved fruitless. Since the night of the ball, the evening before last, he had called twice in Grosvenor Square to see Barton, but both times, Barton had been out. This morning, Chas had decided to stop into a few of Barton's favourite haunts to look for him, but to no avail.

Chas was deeply troubled by what had occurred between Barton and Amanda at that ill-fated gathering. He and Lady Augusta had watched worriedly as the newlyweds quarrelled openly on the dance floor. When the pair disappeared after Cecil and DeValme's arrival, Chas had fervently hoped that they had gone to talk and, perhaps, mend their fences. But when Barton returned to the ballroom, it had been clear that he was more angry than ever. Chas had tried to ask his friend what was amiss, but Barton had only snarled at him and advised him curtly to mind his own affairs.

"Good morning, Mr. Wendover. May I join you?"

Chas Wendover looked up to find Cecil Stratton standing beside his table. Amanda's uncle was dressed in a tight-waisted frock-coat, with a gaudy striped waistcoat underneath; the combination made him look even more overblown and disreputable than was his wont. Chas frowned. He had no desire to pursue a relationship with a man cold-hearted enough to be willing to give his ward to *l'Ange infame,* but common civility forbade him to refuse the older man's request. "Of course," he said grudgingly, and signalled to the waiter. "Should you prefer coffee or tea? Mayhap some chocolate?"

"Brandy, please," Cecil told the servant. "And bring the bottle."

Chas blinked. It was not yet eleven o'clock in the morning.

Cecil noticed his surprise and lied glibly. "I've a bit of a toothache, you see. Can't bear the thought of having it drawn, so I take a brandy now and again to kill the pain."

"I can sympathize," Chas said, straining to make conversation. "I've had a tooth or two turn putrid, and I know how painful it can be."

"That is not my only worry, unfortunately," Cecil continued with a sigh. "I don't scruple to tell you that my dear niece is causing me a bit of concern."

Chas stiffened. "I can't think why," he said coldly.

"All the world must have noticed the lack of amity between my dear Amanda and her husband at the ball," Cecil said. "They danced together but once and barely exchanged a word with each other, so far as I could see. 'Tis very worrisome, very worrisome indeed."

"I do believe that you are making a great deal out of nothing," Chas said uneasily. "They may have had a little spat..."

"My dear Mr. Wendover, a spat does not, typically, lead a gentleman to ignore his bride," Cecil said. "Particularly with all of Society watching!" Cecil gave Chas a sidelong look. "It would not trouble me so, of course," he went on, "did I not already have my doubts as to the strength of their union."

Chas was surprised; he had not thought that Amanda would confide the particulars of her marriage to Cecil. "Indeed?" he said noncommittally.

"You need not fear to discuss the matter with me," Cecil lied. "Amanda has told me all."

Chas shrugged. "One cannot deny that their match came about under the worst of circumstances," he admitted. "But I shouldn't lose hope if I were you. I still believe that the whole thing may work out very nicely."

"You take far more sanguine a view of the matter than I," Cecil said. He was determined to dupe Chas into telling him exactly how Barton and Amanda had come to wed. "I may be old-fashioned," he added cautiously, "but such things were not done in my day."

Chas bridled at the implied criticism. "You should be grateful that your niece ended up in Barton's cabin—it might have turned out very differently for the poor child! Barton did the honourable thing." He hesitated for a moment, then went on, "It never would have happened, had you not put Amanda in a position where she felt that she had no choice but to run away. She would never have stowed away on the *Cumberland Rover* in the first place, had it not been for you. Though it is not my place to say so, you bear a great deal of the blame.''

Cecil did his best to hide his glee. ''Unhappy child,'' he said, shaking his head. ''How sad it is that she should lay the fault for her hasty actions at my door.''

''I don't know whom you'd have her hold accountable,'' Chas said indignantly. ''You were the one who was about to force her into marriage with the Vicomte DeValme. Anyone would fear being wed to such a rotter!''

''I had no intention of forcing Amanda into anything,'' Cecil said primly. ''My niece, as you will learn when you are better acquainted with her, has a habit of... well, exaggerating, one might say. I don't deny that DeValme asked for her hand, nor that I mentioned the offer to Amanda. But that was as far as it went, I promise you.''

''I find that difficult to believe,'' Chas said baldly. ''The poor girl was positively terrified.''

''She was ever a nervous child, much prone to nightmares of all kinds,'' Cecil said. ''I never so much as hinted that she should accept DeValme. Indeed, I should have been quite amazed if she had!''

''Why did you mention the offer to her in the first place, then?'' Chas asked. ''Why didn't you refuse DeValme's offer and send him on his way?''

''To be honest, I thought myself in honour bound to let Amanda decide,'' Cecil explained. ''You must know, Mr. Wendover, that my niece had no dowry, nor expectations of any kind. Since I thought that

DeValme's offer would, in all likelihood, be the only one Amanda would ever receive, it seemed only fair to allow her to make the final choice.''

"There's something in that," Chas admitted. "But Amanda was not left with the impression that it was her decision to make. She truly believed that you would compel her to marry the cad."

Cecil pretended to a remorse he did not feel. "Perhaps, in my concern for her future, I gave Amanda the impression that I wished her to accept DeValme. I can't think how, but it may be that I am to blame for the child's hapless flight." He pushed back his chair and rose from the table. "You will forgive me, sir, I know. I feel that I must go to Amanda and offer her my apologies. How glad I am that we met today, and that we had this little chat! I promise you, I shall take everything you've told me to heart, and I vow that you will see a new beginning between my niece and myself. Good day, Mr. Wendover."

Cecil left the coffee-house smiling. *I have you, Amanda,* he thought smugly. *Thanks to that fool Wendover, you will not dare to defy me now!*

CHAS WENDOVER ELBOWED his way past the bar through a large group of men, all talking excitedly, and moved deeper into the smoky interior of the inn. He found Barton by the tall fireplace, leaning against the mantel and staring into the flames.

"Well met, Bart," he said quietly.

Barton did not look up. "Chas," he responded coolly. "How did you find me?"

"I recalled that there was a prizefight today and thought that you might have decided to drive out to see it. How was it?"

Barton shrugged. "Tolerably entertaining," he said. "The fighters were sufficiently evenly matched to make for an interesting round or two."

A man standing nearby overheard Barton's comment. "Tolerably entertaining?" he exclaimed. "Lord love us, man, they went thirteen rounds, and both of them barely able to stay on their feet by the end!"

"Will you come and join me at a table, where we may speak in private?" Chas asked. Barton shrugged again and moved to join his friend. "I've been looking for you all day, you know," Chas said as they settled themselves. "Since yesterday, in fact! Where have you been?"

"I left the house early yesterday morning, and didn't return until well after midnight," Barton said obliquely. He did not look at Chas. "Have you seen Amanda?"

"Briefly, yesterday morning," Chas answered. He added cautiously, "She is very upset."

"I'm sure your call was more than welcome to her," Barton said. "You no doubt commiserated with her about what a brute I am?"

Chas looked hurt. "We didn't discuss you," he said. "In fact, when I asked Amanda what was wrong, she fobbed me off with some story about a sick headache."

"How very noble of her," Barton drawled.

Chas pushed back his seat. "I'll be off," he said. "I can see that you are in no humour for company, so I shan't impose on you any further."

"That's put me in my place, hasn't it? No, Chas, sit down, sit down!" Barton said ruefully. "My apologies, old friend—I'm in the devil of a mood, but I shouldn't inflict it on you."

Chas hesitated for a moment, then said, "If there's anything you'd like to talk about...?"

Barton laughed harshly. "In point of fact, my boy, the whole reason I was playing least in sight was to avoid talking about it!"

"That is, of course, your privilege," Chas said with dignity.

"Now, there you're wrong," Barton said. "I've shared too much of my life with you not to continue the practice. It's become a habit, you see."

"Well, then..."

Barton paused for a moment, then said, "I don't doubt you noticed that Amanda and I quarrelled during the ball?"

"I dare say the whole ton noticed that!" Chas retorted drily.

Barton grimaced. "Of course they did," he said. "But, believe it or no, that is the least of what concerns me. It's Amanda, Chas. What am I to make of this girl?"

"What happened?" Chas asked.

"She was angry with me because Caro came to the ball. We had a terrible row—Amanda was furious."

"You were angry with her, too," Chas pointed out. "I could see it—you looked the veriest thundercloud!"

"You may lay that at *Monsieur le vicomte*'s door. Amanda knew him! He bowed over her hand and made eyes at her—at my wife, Chas!" Barton shook his head with disgust. "It has me all at sea, I don't mind confessing. Who is she?" He leaned forward, his gaze fixed intently on Chas. "Everything about her is a contradiction. Since we have been married, I have, on the whole, found her to be quiet, modest and an excellent housekeeper. My man of business tells me that she has not touched the allowance I make her— oh, she purchased a new wardrobe, but beyond that she has not spent a groat. And Grandmama could not care more for Amanda had she personally chosen her as my bride."

"I'm dashed fond of Amanda myself," Chas said, not without a certain sheepishness. "She's such a sweet little thing, and so very grateful for the smallest kindness.... I dare say you don't precisely enjoy hearing me sing her praises, do you?"

Barton smiled reluctantly. "It is no surprise," he said. "It was more than passing clear that you'd developed an affection for her. And think of that, Chas—the two people in the world in whom I repose the most trust, yourself and my grandmama, both think very kindly of my wife. That is a point in Amanda's favour, is it not? This is my dilemma, you see. I think of all these things, and then I ask myself—how came she to be on board the *Cumberland Rover?* And how could a gently bred girl possibly be acquainted with *l'Ange infame?*'' He rubbed his face, and Chas saw what a strain the past few weeks had been on him. ''Dash it all, she even went so far as to admit to me that she'd deliberately ensnared me into marriage.''

''It isn't true!'' Chas cried.

Barton stared at his friend. ''How can you be so sure?''

''I only meant...she was very angry with you, you'll recall,'' Chas said uneasily. ''I dare say that you may have spoken a trifle harshly yourself.''

''No, you know something,'' Barton said suspiciously. ''Pray do not trouble to deny it. I'm a trifle too well-acquainted with you to believe your taradiddles.''

''Amanda did confide in me, a little,'' Chas admitted. ''It was when she first came to Town, before you two were even wed. She was so lonely, Bart, and so very unhappy...''

''If she has a story to tell, why didn't she tell me?'' Barton exclaimed. ''If she has some explanation for the ship, and DeValme...''

''Have you given her any reason to believe that her confidences might be welcome to you?'' Chas asked gently. ''Mean to say, you've the devil of a way with you when you're upset!''

Barton was silent for a moment in rueful acknowledgement of Chas's acumen. Then he said, ''You explain it, then. Make sense of this woman for me, won't you?''

''I can't, Bart,'' Chas said. ''I promised!''

"Devil take it, you'd dashed well better..." He stopped and stared at his friend sourly for a long moment. "Very well," he grumbled. "I suppose you're in honour bound not to speak of it." He smiled fleetingly. "Honour does seem to be pricking at me of late, does it not?"

"If only you could be a little kind to Amanda, she'd open her heart to you," Chas said earnestly. "I know she would."

"I have been kind to her," Barton snapped.

"Truly?" Chas's tone was mild.

"Perhaps not so kind as I might have been," Barton admitted grudgingly. Chas said nothing; he only looked at his companion, one eyebrow eloquently raised. Barton laughed reluctantly. "Very well, then, I've been quite horrid at times. Does that satisfy you?"

"It does," Chas said placidly. "And if you wish to continue dwelling in an armed camp, continue your past mode of behaviour, by all means! If, however, you wish to develop a somewhat warmer relationship with Lady Barton...?"

"I don't know," Barton said. "There are times when I think her the most stubborn creature it has ever been my misfortune to encounter." His expression softened. "And yet I cannot deny that I am drawn to her." He looked down at his hand absently; he could almost feel the skin of her shoulder against his palm. "Powerfully drawn!"

"If you are drawn to a lady, and you wish to know more about her, what do you do?" Chas demanded.

"I'm in no mood for guessing games, Chas, and so I warn you."

"You woo her, clunch," Chas said with a grin. "What you must do, my lad, is court your lady wife!"

AMANDA SAT BACK in her seat and put down her needle. It was no use; she had taken up the handwork to distract herself, but no sooner had she set needle to fabric than the same old pictures began chasing through her mind. No matter how she tried to discipline herself not to think of it, or tell herself that she was allowing her imagination to run away with her, images of Carolyn Travers and Barton intruded—laughing, kissing and even indulging in intimacies at which Amanda could only guess. He had had plenty of opportunity to dally with Carolyn, Amanda thought. She had not seen him since the ball.

Why should it trouble her so? she asked herself. At the best of times, gentlemen of fashion were likely to have a *chère amie,* and this was scarcely, she reflected sadly, what one would call the best of times! It was not as though her marriage to Barton were a real one, she told herself. Carolyn could not, in all fairness, have been said to have stolen Barton's affections from her. Indeed, there were many ladies in London in much worse situations than Amanda, for they had married their husbands for love and been forced to suffer their mate's mistresses with as much aplomb as they could muster. Unconsciously, Amanda's hands clenched on the fabric. Had she met and wed Barton in the traditional way, she thought fiercely, she would have walked through fire before she'd have tolerated any such thing!

Amanda had tried to lie to herself, to tell herself that she was only upset about Carolyn because of the gossip it might cause. But now she was too tired and too dispirited to maintain the deception; finally, she was forced to admit to herself that she had fallen in love with her husband. How had it happened? she wondered. When had her feelings for Barton grown so deep? There was no one moment to which she could point. The process had been so gradual, so unconscious that it now seemed to Amanda as though she had loved Barton from the first moment she saw him—or rather, she thought with a blush, from the moment she had landed on top of him in the carriage!

Amanda sighed raggedly. Much good would her feelings do her! she thought bitterly. She had no expectation that her husband would ever return her love. She would be forced to spend the rest of her life hopelessly wishing that Barton would look on her as a true wife, and knowing that it would never happen. It seemed to Amanda as though her misery would choke her, and she buried her face in her hands.

"There is a caller for you," Dennison said.

Amanda looked up sharply. "What?" she said. She had not heard the butler enter the drawing room.

"Mr. Cecil Stratton has come to see you."

"Pray tell him that I am not at..." Amanda began, but the servant turned and left the room before she could finish. She had time only to wipe the final traces of tears from her face before her uncle entered.

"Good day, Amanda," Cecil said cheerfully. "'Tis a glorious morning, is it not?" He regarded his niece and shook his head. "My dear girl, you look the very devil," he said critically. "If you wish to keep that husband of yours happy, you would do well to pay a trifle more attention to your appearance." He puffed a little as he dropped into a chair. "Your husband's happiness is of paramount importance—to both of us."

"What do you want?" Amanda asked wearily.

"Why, only to do you a kindness, my dear," Cecil said, full of *bonhomie*. "Is that not the duty of a doting uncle?"

"It is a role you've avoided quite adroitly so far!"

"Such heat! You should really be more temperate, my dear." Cecil adopted a playfully chiding manner. "I am in the position to grant you a very great favour, I would have you know."

"What favour is that?" Amanda did not trouble to hide her lack of interest.

"Why, the favour of silence," Cecil chuckled. "You have need of it, and I—" he chuckled again "—I chance to have a quantity in stock!"

"What are you talking about?" Amanda demanded.

"I had a most illuminating chat with Chas Wendover this morning. What a tiresome, unpleasant clod he is, to be sure! But he is very much in my good books at the moment, for he chanced to let fall the tale of how you and Barton came to wed. My dear child, I was enthralled!"

Amanda's heart began to hammer in her chest. "And...?"

"Is it not wonderful how the hand of Providence guides us all?" Cecil asked. "Had Wendover not told me the truth, I dare say I might have had a bit of trouble convincing you to give me the money with which to pay DeValme. But as it is, I suspect that you will be more than happy to frank me." He leaned forward. "Imagine, if you will, what the ton would make of such a delicious tale—the proud Lord Barton, caught like a rat in a trap. And what the gossipmongers would say of you—my dear, it does not bear thinking of!"

"You couldn't be so cruel," Amanda said.

"Barton would be the laughing-stock of London, of course," Cecil said. "And you would be reviled. A true lady does not stoop to such methods to catch a husband, as you know."

"I am your own niece!" Amanda cried. "Have you no family feeling? Would you really humiliate me so?"

Cecil shrugged. "I would go a great deal further than this to keep DeValme from my throat," he said. "And, really, my dear, it's all your own fault. Had you done as you were told, and married the *vicomte*, none of this ever would have happened." He regarded Amanda with a benign smile. "Now... when may I expect my money?"

"I have none to give you!" Amanda said wildly. "Why won't you believe me?"

Cecil tut-tutted. "Pray do not play me for a fool," he said. "Barton must have made you an allowance."

"I . . . I swore to him that I would never touch it," Amanda said. "I will not break my vow."

"Your vows, and whether or not you break them, are not of the slightest interest to me," Cecil said. "But I'm sorry to say that your dilemma is a trifle greater than you realize! While I'm certain that Barton has made generous allowance for your needs, I fear that between what I owe to DeValme and my own more pressing obligations, I shall require a deal more than what you likely have in your account." He named a sum that made Amanda gasp.

"You might just as well ask for the moon," she said bitterly. "How could I ever raise that amount?"

"Why not sell your jewellery?" Cecil suggested practically. "That emerald necklace you were wearing the other evening would fetch a pretty price, I have no doubt, and I dare say you've many other costly pieces at your disposal."

"What jewels I have are family heirlooms," Amanda said miserably. "I couldn't possibly. . ."

"Well," Cecil said briskly as he rose from his seat, "where you find the blunt is really no concern of mine, is it? And, as an act of avuncular kindness, I shall give you a little time to raise the ready. But do not think to cross me, my dear," he warned her as he made ready to leave, "lest you find yourself a social outcast, and your husband the butt of every joke from Oxford Street to Piccadilly!"

CHAPTER ELEVEN

BARTON PAUSED outside the morning-room, took a deep breath, adjusted his neckcloth and entered. "Good morning, Amanda," he said.

Amanda froze in the process of pouring herself a cup of tea, her expression so comically alarmed that Barton burst out laughing. "My dear, you needn't look at me so!" he said. "I've only come to take breakfast with you."

"My lord, I..." Amanda swallowed. "I was not expecting you."

"That," he answered drily, "is quite evident."

"May I...may I pour you some tea?" Amanda did not meet his eyes.

"Thank you, I should very much like some," Barton said. He fixed himself a plate and slid into a seat across from Amanda.

"I can't think what is keeping Lady Augusta," Amanda said nervously. "She's usually down long before this."

"My grandmother," Barton said, "was kind enough to agree to take a tray in her room this morning. I told her that I wished to be private with my wife, you see."

"You...you did?" Amanda began to pleat her napkin between her fingers.

"Yes. There are matters that we ought to discuss, wouldn't you agree?" Barton did not wait for Amanda to answer him. "First of all, I wish to apologize for Carolyn Travers's behaviour," he said quietly. "She has treated you quite execrably, and for that, I am truly sorry." He grinned ruefully. "I didn't invite her to the ball, but I should have realized that the lack of an invitation would not stop her. Caro is the most headstrong of creatures!"

Amanda's mouth twisted bitterly. "She had good reason to believe that she would be welcome here, did she not?"

"No, she did not," Barton said flatly. "Carolyn knew that I would not enjoy her company—I had made that quite clear to her." He paused, then added, "Or so I thought!"

"You...you had?"

"Not to put too fine a point on it, I had severed all connections with Lady Travers before ever you and I met," Barton said. He toyed with his cup for a moment, then raised his eyes and met Amanda's gaze squarely. "It's terribly improper of me to tell you so, but...I wanted you to know."

"Thank you, my lord," Amanda said. "It is generous in you to be so frank." She essayed a smile. "After all, it is really none of my concern, is it?"

"I should not say that," Barton said. "However it came to pass, we did marry. You have the right not to be embarrassed, or made to feel self-conscious." He hesitated for a moment, then cleared his throat. "About the ball..."

"I'm glad that you mentioned it," she said. She looked up and met Barton's gaze earnestly. "I behaved inexcusably."

Barton was impressed by her honesty. "You were very angry!" he said gently.

Amanda nodded, shamefaced. "It was ridiculous, I know, but after all that Lady Travers said..." She shook her head. "But that is no excuse. I am sorry!"

Barton grinned crookedly. "You mustn't blame yourself too much. I was rather intemperate myself, as I recall!"

"I can't imagine what you must think of me." Amanda shuddered. "The things I said...!"

"I propose that we do our best, both of us, to pretend that that cursed ball was never held," Barton suggested. "What do you say, Amanda? Shall we ignore the whole ugly incident?"

Amanda smiled shyly at her husband. "Indeed, my lord, that seems an excellent notion to me!"

Barton propped his chin on his hand, and regarded his bride with a frown. "Do you know, Amanda, there is one habit you have that annoys me to distraction?"

Amanda paled. "What... what is that, my lord?" she asked hesitantly.

"This infernal habit of yours of sprinkling every other sentence with 'my lord.'" His eyes twinkling, he went on, "I promise you, my dear, I am not so jealous of my position that I insist upon my own wife addressing me by my title! Could you not call me Barton—or, better yet, Bart? I shan't ask you to call me Will, lest you think that I've lost all sense of my own consequence.''

Amanda laughed delightedly. ''Very well, my... Bart,'' she said.

''Very good.'' He nodded briskly. ''There's one more thing that I should like to ask you,'' he went on. ''Will you attend the opera with me this evening?''

Amanda's face lit up. ''The opera?'' she breathed. ''Oh, Bart, I should love to!'' Barton saw the glow on her face and felt a strange tightness in his chest. ''You don't know how I've longed to go to the opera, and to the theatre,'' she continued. ''It will be such fun!'' Her expression sobered. ''But are you sure that you wish to?'' she asked doubtfully. ''Would you not find it more agreeable to go with your friends?''

For a brief moment, Barton covered Amanda's hand with his own. ''I promise you, my dear,'' he said, ''there is nothing I should rather do than take you to the opera!'' And he found, much to his own surprise, that he spoke no more than the truth.

LADY AUGUSTA tapped softly on Amanda's door. ''Amanda?'' she called. ''May I come in?''

The door opened, and Amanda all but pulled Barton's grandmother into her bedchamber. ''Thank goodness you're here,'' Amanda said breathlessly. ''I am in such a muddle!''

Lady Augusta's heart sank. ''Drat that boy!'' she exclaimed. ''You must pay him no mind, child. Unfortunately, he takes too much after me—he speaks first, then stops to think.''

Amanda looked as though she might burst into tears. "He ... he does?"

"He has the very devil of a temper! I dare say he didn't mean a word he said." Lady Augusta stepped farther into the room and observed that what appeared to be every stitch of clothing that Amanda owned was spread out about the room. "Oh, no, my dear, you mustn't!" she cried. "I knew that I should never have let him persuade me to take breakfast in my room. But no matter how harsh he has been, you must not leave him, child. You don't know how cruel the ton can be—you would be positively crucified."

Amanda shook her head. "What?"

"You must reside here, with Bart," Lady Augusta said. "But I shall speak to him, I promise you. You need have no fear that my grandson will continue to plague you."

Amanda sank weakly onto a footstool. "I think," she said shakily, "that you are labouring under a misapprehension, my lady."

"Perhaps I am," Lady Augusta said slowly. "Please, my dear, won't you tell me what passed between you and Bart this morning?"

"Oh, my lady, he was so very kind!" Amanda said eagerly. "He apologized to me for Carolyn Travers's appearance at the ball and told me that he should not have spoken to me as he did. Then he invited me to attend the opera with him this evening." She smiled ruefully up at Lady Augusta. "That is why I am in such a muddle, you see. I can't think what to wear!"

Lady Augusta clapped her hands. "But this is marvellous! Has that stubborn rapscallion finally come to his senses?"

Amanda's smile wavered. "You mustn't make too much of this," she warned Lady Augusta. "I dare say Bart only wishes to come to a more . . . more workable arrangement between us."

"Nonsense, child," Lady Augusta scoffed. "He's beginning to see what a beautiful, fetching creature you are—and past time, too."

"Lady Augusta!" Amanda protested, blushing furiously.

"No missishness if you please," the elderly woman retorted. "You cannot tell me that you are not madly in love with your husband—I've eyes to see with, my dear, and I don't take kindly to taradiddles." Amanda did not speak, but the expression on her face made Lady Augusta snort triumphantly. "Just as I thought!" She nodded, satisfied.

"My feelings for Barton do not change anything," Amanda said quietly. "He may have come to regard me in a somewhat kinder light, but he will never learn to love me."

"He may not love you yet," Lady Augusta acknowledged. "But, if you will agree that I know the boy a trifle better than you do, you will believe me when I tell you that he could!" She thoughtfully regarded the wardrobe spread about the room. "But we must help him to see you in as flattering a light as possible. Show me your gowns, my dear, and I shall help you to choose the right one."

Amanda proceeded to spend the next hour or more modelling various ensembles for her critical grandmother-in-law. Finally the two women settled on a simply styled gown, made of a rich rust-coloured velvet that brought out the red highlights in Amanda's hair and made her brown eyes glow.

"That will do very nicely," Lady Augusta said, satisfied. "And you must wear the family diamond-and-emerald coronet. It is quite shockingly vulgar, but it will make you look an absolute princess."

Amanda clasped Lady Augusta's hands. "How can I ever thank you for all your kindnesses to me?" she asked.

Lady Augusta returned the grip warmly. "You do know that I've come to love you, don't you, child?" she asked. Amanda nodded, blinking back tears. "Then you may thank me by doing me a small favour," she said. "Tell Bart about yourself—tell him how you came to be on the ship that night, and how you come to know such a scoundrel as the Vicomte DeValme."

"I'm...I'm afraid," Amanda said. "I've wanted to tell him, but I did try once before, you know. He didn't believe me. What if he still won't?" She shivered. "I don't think that I could bear it," she finished sadly.

"Of course he will believe you," Lady Augusta said definitely.

"How can you know that?" Amanda asked with the ghost of a smile. "You do not know the story yourself—let me tell you, Grandmama!" The word slipped out before Amanda realized it.

Lady Augusta smiled and gently stroked Amanda's hair. "I do not need to hear it," she said. "I am an old woman, and I've learned one thing in life—good people rarely do awful things. When they do, it is generally because they have no choice." She lifted Amanda's chin. "I don't need to hear it," she repeated. "But Barton does! He is a gentleman, and to gentlemen, pride is everything. He needs to know that it was Fate that brought you two together, and not some sort of nefarious scheme on your part. Then he may let go of his pride and welcome you into his life."

"Do you really think . . . ?"

"I do, child." Lady Augusta nodded. "If you will only open your heart to Barton, I believe that you will be quite flabbergasted by the result."

AMANDA CAME DOWN the great double staircase slowly, her eyes shyly lowered. Barton, watching her descent from the foot of the stairs, thought wonderingly that he had never seen anything so beautiful in all his days. She positively glowed! The faint colour in her cheeks made her skin appear all the more creamy, and, when she finally looked up, the diamond-and-emerald coronet nestled in her hair was no brighter than the stars in her eyes.

"My dear Amanda," he said, and swept a low bow. "You are breathtaking!"

Amanda's colour deepened faintly. "Thank you, my . . . Bart," she said, then asked artlessly, "Do you really like it?"

"It was worth every penny of the undoubtedly considerable sum that I paid for it," he told her with an infectious grin.

Amanda laughed. "It was rather dear," she allowed, smoothing the fabric of the gown. "But Mrs. Mandley said that you would wish me to be well attired."

"She was absolutely right. If every gown you purchase looks so charmingly on you, you may spend every groat I have on clothing with my very best wishes," Barton said grandly.

Amanda laughed again, and Barton felt suddenly, absurdly happy. "Shall we go?" he asked, offering Amanda his arm.

When they were settled in their carriage and on their way, Amanda asked what opera they would see.

"La Cenerentola," he replied.

Amanda wrinkled her nose. "I'm afraid I don't..."

"You may be more familiar with it than you think," Barton said. "It is from a story by M. Charles Perrault, called *Cinderella.*"

"Cinderella?" Amanda clapped her hands. "But that is one of my favorite tales!"

"The opera made its debut in Rome last year," Barton said. "It happened that I was there at the time and saw the opening. I think you will enjoy it."

Before much more time had passed, they had arrived, and Barton was escorting Amanda into the lobby of the King's Theatre. As they entered, Barton looked over Amanda's shoulder, and a broad grin spread across his face. "Brace yourself, my dear," he murmured. "You are in for a rare treat!"

Amanda turned and observed a tall, cadaverous-looking gentleman mincing towards them. He was dressed all in yellow; even his evening coat was made of a bright, primrose satin. On his feet he wore the high, red-heeled shoes that had been popular in what must have been his grandfather's time, for the man himself looked to be no more than twenty-five or thirty.

"Well met, Barton!" he exclaimed as he joined them. "I had hoped to see you here this evening. I was quite devastated to have missed your ball, *mon ami,* but my lady was just delivered of *un petit paquet,* and I thought it only right that I should stay in the country to support her through her travail." He turned to Amanda and swept her a deep bow. "Good evening," he said politely.

Barton, eyes twinkling, said, "Amanda, this is my very good friend Lord Acton. Acton, my wife, Lady Barton."

Lord Acton bowed again. "I can see," he said, "that rumour did not lie!"

Amanda's hand tightened on Barton's sleeve, but Barton's smile remained steady. "How so, my friend?"

"They told me that your bride was a veritable beauty, a diamond of the first water, but I see that the gossip-mongers did not do her justice! One can only wonder how you ever convinced this charming lady to wed you. You must surely be the most charitable of creatures, Lady Barton, to have agreed to spend your life with this dolt."

Amanda smiled shyly at Lord Acton. "Indeed, my lord," she said softly, "there are many who might think me the lucky one!"

Acton made a rude noise. "No one acquainted with Barton," he said, "would ever think anything so ridiculous!" He glanced over his shoulder. "I shall bid you adieu," he said. "I've escorted my grandmama here this evening, and she is, I promise you, the most impatient of harridans. Had I not expectations from her... but no matter. Good evening, fair Lady Barton! We shall meet again soon, I have no doubt. Barton, do try not to give this charming lady too much of a disgust for you before I have the chance to come to know her better. Good evening!" He bowed over Amanda's hand again and minced away.

"How very... very kind, to be sure," Amanda said faintly.

"Don't let appearances deceive you," Barton said dryly. "Acton is a bruising rider to hounds, a fiery member of the House of Lords and the father of a family of five—and only six years wed!" Barton chuckled. "He also enjoys a relationship of the utmost warmth with his grandmother."

"Is he really your very good friend?" Amanda asked.

"Second only to Chas," Barton said. "And his opinion makes it unanimous—everyone I know thinks me a lucky dog to have won such a beauty!"

Amanda was spared the necessity of answering by the sound of a soft gong, which indicated that the opera was about to begin.

"Shall we go in?" Once again Barton offered his arm to Amanda, then he escorted her into his box.

Barton was something of a music lover, and he had attended the opera many times. But never, he thought, had he enjoyed it so much as he did this night, in the company of his bride. He did not watch the stage, but, rather, Amanda, who was completely oblivious of his regard. Once the performance began, the girl was swept away. She sat perched on the edge of her gilt chair, her eyes sparkling, swaying ever so gently in time with the music. At the end of the first act, when Cinderella arrived at the ball, radiant in all her finery, Amanda's mouth opened in a soundless sigh of admiration.

After the curtain had fallen for intermission and the thunder of applause had died down, Barton leaned forward. "Are you enjoying yourself, my dear?"

"Oh, Bart, it is wonderful," Amanda breathed. "I have never had such a wonderful night—never! How can I ever thank you?"

Barton looked deep into Amanda's eyes. "I can think of a way," he said huskily. He slipped one hand around Amanda's waist and gently lowered his lips to hers.

The kiss, which had begun as a gentle salute, stretched on and on. Barton had the curious fancy that he and Amanda were alone, just the two of them on an empty, beautiful planet. One of Amanda's hands crept up to clutch at his lapel, and his grip on her waist tightened.

"But how very charming," Cecil Stratton purred. "A tender moment between newlyweds?" He had entered their box unnoticed and now stood smiling fatuously at the pair.

Barton was hard put to bite back a curse. He moved away from his wife and nodded curtly at her uncle. "Stratton," he said.

"How very lucky you are that you are able to afford a private box, Barton," Cecil said. "Else you and your pretty bride might be subject to all manner of stares when you, ah, demonstrate your affection." He settled himself down, and added, "Alas! I am at present unable to support such an extravagance, I fear. I'm forced to watch from the floor, and very unpleasant I find it, to be sure. How lowering it is to be cast among *hoi polloi* when one has grown accustomed to the heights! It is a situation which I pray you two shall never experience." He stared challengingly at his niece. "Happily, I hope soon to be able to live in a manner more befitting my birth. Isn't that so, Amanda?"

The girl did not look up, but murmured an incoherent response. The colour which had flamed into her cheeks on Cecil's arrival had faded, leaving her pale and with an apprehensive expression.

Barton frowned, not really listening to Cecil. Why should Amanda suddenly look so unhappy? Had his kiss frightened her? He would have sworn that she had enjoyed it just as much as he had—and he had!—but perhaps his ardour had alarmed her.

"Yes, it has been most difficult living in straitened circumstances," Cecil continued, enjoying Amanda's discomfiture. "But all is well that ends well, and I do believe that everything may turn out for the best."

"Indeed," Barton said absently, his attention still focussed on Amanda.

Cecil rose. "Well, I'll leave you now to enjoy your privacy," he said. "I only wished to look in for a moment to pay my respects. Good evening, my lord. Amanda, I shall speak to you very soon, my dear." With a bow, he was gone.

"Amanda, is something—" Barton began, but the peal of the gong interrupted him; the opera was about to resume. Barton regarded his wife for a moment more with a troubled frown but held his peace.

Amanda sat with her eyes riveted to the stage, but could not, afterwards, have described a single thing that occurred in the second act. She felt as if at any moment she might burst into hysterical laughter, or, perhaps, dissolve into tears. This evening had begun so perfectly. At the moment Barton's lips had touched hers, she had felt as though she had won a marvellous, rare prize, one that she did not deserve. For one magical moment, she had believed that Barton might be learning to care for her, and the thought had made her dizzy with joy.

Then Cecil Stratton had arrived and reminded Amanda of what might still happen. If he were to tell the tale of Lord and Lady Barton's meeting and marriage to the ton, the ensuing gossip would sound the death-knell for whatever feelings Barton might be beginning to develop for her. Amanda knew that a man as proud as her husband could never bear to be the butt of the *haut monde*'s jokes. He would hate her for it, and could she really blame him?

But what was her alternative? How could she possibly raise the inordinate sum that Cecil had demanded of her? Her mind went round and round the problem as the second act progressed, but she was no nearer to a solution when the final curtain was rung down.

Barton escorted her out to their carriage in silence. It was not until they were seated and on their way home that Barton asked softly, "Amanda? Are you angry with me?"

Amanda realized with a shock that she had not spoken a word to Barton since Cecil's arrival in the box. "Oh, no," she said. "How could I be?"

"Did I alarm you when I...that is to say, that kiss was..."

"It did not frighten me at all!" Amanda blurted out, then blushed furiously.

"I'm glad," Barton said. Amanda could hear the smile in his voice. "But if it was not the kiss that upset you, what was it? Was it Cecil?"

"Ye...no," Amanda said unconvincingly.

Barton opened his mouth to probe further, but thought better of it. He paused for a moment, then went on in a cheerful voice, "Did you enjoy the opera?"

"Oh, yes," Amanda said. "I don't know how I can ever thank you for such a pleasant evening. It was kind of you to treat me as though we were really...as though our marriage were..." She stopped and blinked back the tears that had filled her eyes. "You will never know," she finished simply, "what this evening has meant to me."

There was a long silence, then Barton reached over and took her hand in his strong clasp. "Amanda," he said, "won't you tell me how you came to be aboard the *Cumberland Rover* that night?"

CHAPTER TWELVE

AMANDA CAME DOWN the stairs humming. "Good morning, Dennison," she said, able this morning to smile even at the butler whom she so disliked. "Is his lordship in the morning-room?"

"No," the servant said. "Lord Barton sends you his compliments and says that he will be home for nuncheon. He's gone to his club."

Amanda blushed. "And Lady Augusta?" she asked.

"I believe that she had an appointment with her modiste." Dennison stared at a point somewhere over Amanda's head. "Will there be anything else, madam?" he finished insolently.

"Yes, Dennison, there will," Amanda said, taking her courage in her hands. "In future, you will be so good as to address me by my title."

Dennison opened his mouth to speak, but Amanda stared at him implacably. He finally mumbled, "Yes, my lady."

"Very good," she said briskly. "Now, if you please, have Cook send up some fresh toast and tea. I have a powerful hunger today!" She turned away and did not see the blazing look of hatred on Dennison's face.

As she made her way to the morning-room, Amanda could not help but smile. What a beautiful morning it was! she thought, then chuckled. Had it been pouring rain, she would have considered it the most glorious of days, for she and Barton had come to a new understanding.

Last night, when Barton had asked her how she had chanced to be on board the ship from France, for a moment Amanda had felt blind panic. Then she had remembered both Chas and Lady Augusta urging her to be frank with her husband, and she had somehow found the strength to stammer out her tale. Barton had listened in silence. When she had come to the end, he did not speak for so long that she had begun to be afraid that she had made a terrible mistake.

Then, finally, he had said, "My God, Amanda— how you must have loathed me for being so certain that you had only set out to trap me!"

Amanda had essayed a smile in the dimness of the carriage. "At first I did," she confessed. "I thought you insufferable in your conceit, to be perfectly honest! But once I came to realize how much your honour meant to you and what lengths you would go to to protect your family...I realized that perhaps you were not as top-lofty as I had imagined."

"You are very charitable," he had said. "Too charitable, I fear. What was it you called me—'insufferable in my own conceit?' How truly you spoke! When I think of the things I said to you...the way I behaved! How can you bear the sight of me, child?"

"You must not take all the blame," Amanda had said earnestly. "I should have told you long ago, but I was too proud, foolishly proud."

"Well, I will allow that I wish you had been open with me much sooner, if only so that I might have avoided making quite such a fool of myself," Barton had said ironically. "But that is not important now." He had been silent for a long moment, then continued, "I begin to see why Cecil's presence this evening should have so distressed you. The man is . . . well, in deference to you I shan't say what he is, but he has treated you quite abominably. And DeValme . . ." Amanda had sensed, rather than seen, his frown. "That rotter, to think of wedding an innocent girl!"

Amanda had recalled DeValme's words to her and said, fair-mindedly, "In truth, the *vicomte* did not press me in any way to marry him. And I must admit that he has been most gentlemanly since he arrived in London."

"Don't let his pleasant demeanor fool you," Barton said drily. "He uses Cecil as his cat's-paw, and then disclaims any knowledge of your uncle's sins. But we shall waste no more time speaking of those two. Amanda . . . I am sorry! I behaved abominably to you, and all because I was too stubborn to give you the benefit of the doubt. Can you forgive me?"

"There's naught to forgive," Amanda had shyly answered. "Had I not been so stubborn . . ."

Barton had laughed, the sound like a caress in the darkness. "Shall we agree that there was more than enough foolishness between the two of us to go round?"

The rest of the ride home had passed quickly, with Amanda in a fog of happiness. When they reached Grosvenor Square, Barton had escorted Amanda to her room and pressed a lingering kiss onto her hand. "Until tomorrow," he had said, and it had seemed to his wife that his smile was full of promise.

Amanda sighed happily and entered the morning-room. She had no sooner settled herself at the table when Dennison entered, bearing a silver salver with her tea and toast, and a folded piece of notepaper. "A letter's come for you, my lady," he said sullenly. He set her breakfast before her, laid the paper beside her tea cup and departed.

Amanda curiously turned the note over in her fingers. She did not recognize the crabbed handwriting. Who could be writing to her? She shrugged and opened the missive. "My dear Amanda," it began.

How lovely it was to see you at the opera last night, and how I enjoyed watching you flirt with your husband! How very wise of you, my dear, to tie Barton to you with chains of affection—they are so pleasant to forge, and very much the hardest of bonds to break! And they will make it that much the easier for you to beguile the money you so desperately need from him.

While we are on the subject of filthy lucre, I regret to inform you that I can give you no more than another two days to reimburse me for the expenses I have incurred on your behalf. Do not, pray, waste my time or yours on more vain attempts to plead for mercy; it is a luxury which,

alas, I cannot afford. If I do not hear from you,
you may rest assured that the ton will hear my
story told, and in the most lurid and unflattering
of terms!

Yours, etc.,
Cecil Stratton

Amanda sat motionless, the paper clutched tight in
her hands. Two days! she thought, stunned. How in
heaven's name was she to put her hand to such a vast
sum of money in only two days? She bent her mind to
the problem, frantic to find a solution. Perhaps she
should just tell Barton of Cecil's demands. Before the
idea was fully formulated, she rejected it. The new-
found accord between herself and her husband was so
tenuous that she dared not risk it by revealing the
depth of her uncle's corruption. For Barton, a man to
whom family was all-important, the notion that Cecil
Stratton would not scruple to blackmail his own niece
would be abhorrent.

And there was no point in importuning her uncle
again, she thought bitterly. Cecil had made it quite
clear that he had no finer sensibilities to be appealed
to! He would do his best to humiliate Barton if she did
not find the means to pay him.

She shuddered at the thought of Barton's reaction,
should the ton learn what had happened that night on
the *Cumberland Rover.* He would be mortified; the
giggles and sneers of the *haut monde* would cut Barton like a knife. And what would be his reaction?
Amanda could not but believe that he would come to
loathe her.

Amanda crumpled the note in her fist and stared off into space, her mind working furiously. When Dennison re-entered the room she stared at him blankly.

"A caller for you, my lady," he said. "The Vicomte DeValme."

"Tell him that I am not..." Amanda began, then stopped. She thought for a minute, then straightened her shoulders. "Be so good as to see him into the drawing-room, please," she said. "I'll join him in just a moment."

After Dennison left, Amanda remained seated at the morning-room table for a long moment, her brow furrowed in a frown. Then she rose and made her way upstairs.

When Amanda entered the drawing room, DeValme was standing by the window, staring out into the square. He turned as the door closed behind her. "My dear Amanda," he said, crossing to join her. "How do you do?"

"Not very well, I'm afraid," Amanda said honestly. "I am very troubled, in fact."

"Oh?" DeValme escorted his hostess to a seat, then sat down across from her. "Perhaps I might be of some assistance."

"It may be that you can," Amanda said, and wondered at her own boldness. "May I be open with you, my lord?"

DeValme gestured gracefully. "But of course, my dear!" he said.

Amanda knotted her hands in her lap. "It is my uncle," she began.

DeValme smiled. "He is a heavy burden to you, I have no doubt! It seems quite remarkable that both of you should spring from the same family, for two creatures less alike I have never met."

Amanda smiled perfunctorily. "I have learned," she said, "that my uncle owes you a certain sum of money."

DeValme frowned. "May I ask," he said, feigning displeasure, "how you came to learn of it?"

"Cecil told me," Amanda said. "In fact, he—"

"He should never have mentioned it to you," DeValme said heavily. "A lady's sensibilities are far too refined to be sullied by matters of finance. I can only apologize to you for his gaucherie."

"You don't understand," Amanda said. "Cecil holds me responsible for the debt. He says that he should never have owed you anything, had...had you and I wed."

"But this is absurd," DeValme lied. "Your uncle's indebtedness to me has nothing whatever to do with you. It is, in fact, a matter of honour."

"He lost money to you at play?"

"Precisely." DeValme nodded. "So you see that you may cheerfully tell him to go to the devil!"

Amanda shook her head sadly. "It is not so simple as that, I fear. He seems quite determined to make me pay."

"Ah, all becomes clear now!" DeValme exclaimed. "He is plaguing you, I take it?"

"You have no idea," Amanda replied fervently. "He can be very...persistent!"

"But this is of a matter the simplest," DeValme said. "Since your terrible uncle seems determined to torment you, I shall tell him that I forgive him his debt. Will that make you happy, little one?"

Amanda's face lit up. "Oh, yes!" she said. "I should blush to admit it, I know, but I had hoped that you might...oh!" Her face fell.

"What is it, Amanda?" DeValme asked.

Amanda had recalled, too late, that Cecil had told her that his debts involved more than just what he owed to DeValme. He had specifically mentioned wishing to pay off the "more pressing" of his obligations. Would it make any difference to Cecil if DeValme did forgive what Cecil owed him? Amanda thought not.

"What is it?" DeValme asked again.

"Nothing," Amanda said. "I thank you for your generous offer, my lord, but it will not serve."

DeValme regarded Amanda for a moment, then, still watching her closely, said, "My dear, if your uncle is truly making such a nuisance of himself, why not tell Barton? I promise you, your husband is more than adequately equipped to deal with such a one as Cecil Stratton!"

"No!" Amanda cried. Then she added, more moderately, "That is to say, I don't wish to trouble Barton with it."

DeValme schooled his features to an expression of gravity and said, "Well, if you will not tell your husband, and you do not wish me to forgive Cecil's debt, what may I do to help you?"

"There is nothing you can do," Amanda said. "Indeed, I should never have mentioned the matter to you."

"Nonsense," DeValme said. "Have I not told you that I should like to stand your friend? It has become an object with me to bask in your good graces, and I am quite determined to do so!"

Amanda could not help but recall the fear that the French peer had always inspired in her. "Why should you be so very kind to me?" she asked bluntly.

"I promise you, child, I am not the villain that you think me. Let me show you . . . only let me demonstrate what a good friend I can be!"

"I thank you for the offer," Amanda said. "But I shall deal with the matter myself. There is naught that you can do, my lord."

"That," DeValme responded, "remains to be seen!" He rose and bowed over her hand. "Trust in me, little one," he said. "I shall not fail you!"

The *vicomte* could not contain a smirk of satisfaction as he shut the drawing-room door behind him, and a silent chuckle shook his shoulders as he reached the head of the stairs. As he began his descent, he saw Dennison admitting Cecil Stratton; the two were deep in conversation. DeValme was about to hail Amanda's uncle when he noticed Barton coming out of his library and into the hall, so he stepped back into the shadows at the head of the stairs.

"Stratton!" Barton called. He had his gloves and hat in his hand; he had, apparently, just returned home.

"My lord!" Cecil said with an oily smile. "How do you do?"

"Dennison, that will be all," Barton said. He waited until the servant had left the hall before continuing. "You will do me the favour, Stratton, of staying away from this house, if you please."

"What? I don't understand," Cecil said.

"Allow me to make myself abundantly clear, then," Barton said coldly. "You are not welcome here, or anywhere else where my wife and I may reside."

"How dare you speak to me so?" Cecil blustered. "Amanda will have something to say to you about this, my lord. Of that you may be sure!"

"I dare say she will. Her thanks will be positively deafening, I have no doubt!" Barton said. "The manner in which you have treated her is...well, appalling is too light a word, I think. You have behaved infamously, and you may credit the affection I bear Amanda for the fact that I do not call you out for it." Barton crossed the hall and opened the front door. "Good day, Stratton," he said.

Cecil opened and shut his mouth several times before any sound emerged. "You shall be sorry for this, Barton," he squeaked. "You shall be sorry!"

Barton slammed the outside door shut behind Cecil and returned to his library. DeValme waited only until the library door had closed in its turn before nipping down the stairs and out of doors, where he soon caught up with Cecil Stratton.

"What ho, *mon vieux?*" he said, grinning broadly. "Barton has given you a rare dressing-down, has he not?"

Cecil's round face was flushed with colour. "Did you hear him?" he cried. "That arrogant, overbearing young puppy! That he should dare..."

"Did I not tell you so?" DeValme asked. "He must be humbled, that one." The *vicomte* hailed a hackney cab and directed the driver to his lodgings. "Never fear, Cecil," he continued after they had settled themselves in the conveyance. "We are on the verge of tasting our revenge." He chuckled. "It is deliciously piquant, my friend. Do you know that your niece actually turned to me for help in finding the money to pay you off?" Cecil stared open-mouthed at the Frenchman as DeValme went on. "But yes, my friend, I promise you, 'tis true!"

"Has she run mad?" Cecil asked. "Doesn't she realize...?"

"Apparently not," DeValme said. "Which is all to the good, of course."

"We are still agreed, are we not, that if you are able...that is to say, if I help you to..." Cecil began anxiously.

"If you play my henchman, Cecil, I shall forgive your debt," DeValme said. "That was our agreement."

"So if she pays me, too..."

"There is no chance of that," DeValme said, "which is why I had you ask her for so much more than you owe me—to make it impossible for her to be able to raise the money. In her desperation, I had hoped that she might make herself vulnerable to me, and so she has!"

Cecil brightened. "What do you want me to do, then?" he asked.

"For the moment, nothing," DeValme replied. "You did well, *mon vieux*. That letter you sent put Amanda into the perfect state of mind to confide in me, and I ask no more of you than that, for the moment at least. When the time comes, you will have an important part to play! But for now I believe I shall go and call on the beautiful Carolyn. It is almost time for her role to begin."

"I don't see why you need her," Cecil said.

"Why, for her excellent relationship with Dennison, Lord Barton's butler," DeValme said. "Did you know that she has been bribing him for months? At first it was to keep her informed of his master's movements. Lately, of course, that has changed. How did you think she managed to be admitted to the ball? A handsome vail, *et voilà!* the thing is done. When the time comes, she will be of great help to us—she can enlist this servant's aid. And if, perchance, he tries to refuse, she need only threaten to expose his perfidy to his master to force him to go along with us."

"You do seem to have thought of everything," Cecil said admiringly.

"I have," DeValme said smugly. "When it comes to matters of retribution, I leave nothing to chance." He sat back in his seat. "For my mills grind slowly, my dear Cecil, but exceedingly fine!"

AMANDA PUSHED UP the sleeves of the voluminous white smock she wore over her clothing and motioned to the maid. "Do be careful, Mary!" she said.

"That is a Sèvres figurine, and very delicate. Dust it gently, if you please."

The servant bobbed her head and carefully continued to clean the bric-a-brac that stood on the drawing-room mantel. Amanda turned her attention to the other maid, who was struggling to take down the heavy damask draperies that hung at the window. "Here, let me help you," she said briskly, and climbed up on a stool, straining to reach the end of the rod.

The drawing-room door opened, and Lord Barton entered. "What on earth... Amanda, what are you doing?"

Amanda started at the sound of his voice, and the heavy curtains slipped from her hands. The heavy fabric landed on the floor with a thump, and a cloud of dust rose up to envelop Amanda, the maid and Barton.

Amanda ineffectually attempted to wave the dust away. "We are only giving this room a good turning-out, my lord," she said guiltily. "You can see that it is in desperate need of a thorough cleaning!"

"My dear girl, there's no need for you to look so absurdly contrite," Barton said, amused. "I'm sure your housewifely fervour does you credit, though I should have thought that these good ladies—" he smiled at the maids "—could have managed the thing without your help."

Amanda looked away. It had ever been her habit, when troubled or upset, to find such tasks to do as would keep her thoroughly distracted. And she had never, she thought, been so troubled as she was at the moment! Between Cecil's threats and the fact that she was beginning to deeply regret ever telling DeValme of her problems, she had begun to think that she might go mad if she did not find some way to occupy herself.

"Indeed, my lady," said one of the maids, emboldened by Barton's words, "we could finish up in here in a trice. We've only to finish dusting and take these curtains out to be beaten, and we'll be well nigh done."

"And I should like a moment or two of your time if you don't mind," Barton said smoothly.

Amanda hesitated for a moment, then shrugged. "Very well," she said. "Mary, I shall rely on you to see to it that everything is in apple-pie order—and before tea, please." Barton helped his wife remove her smock, then led her out of the room.

"Shall we go out into the garden?" he asked. "It is a beautiful afternoon."

"Very well, my..."

Barton held a finger against her lips. "I thought we had agreed," he said, mock-sternly, "that there would be no more of that 'my lord' nonsense?"

Amanda could not help but laugh. "Yes, Barton," she said with feigned contrition.

"Much better," he responded approvingly. He held the garden door open for her, and they commenced to stroll down the path that led through Barton's small Town garden.

"How very beautiful it is," Amanda said admiringly. "Your gardener has done a marvellous job, and in such a limited space, too! One might think oneself in the middle of the country."

"Yes, he has contrived to create a wonderfully secluded spot, has he not?" Barton helped Amanda to a bench surrounded by rose-bushes. "The perfect place for a bit of dalliance, I've always thought."

Amanda blushed and seated herself gingerly on the bench.

"Not that I've tested my belief, you understand," he continued, seating himself very close to her. "At least, not until now."

Amanda's blush deepened, and she moved slightly away from him.

"Be careful, my pet," Barton said, grinning, "lest you fall right off!"

"Was there...was there something in particular that you wished to discuss, Barton?" she asked nervously.

"There was," he said. He began to toy with the lace that hung from Amanda's sleeve. She was hard put to contain a shiver as his fingers brushed against her arm. "Our marriage did not have a terribly propitious start, did it?" he asked. "But however it may have begun, married we are, Amanda, and married we shall stay." He paused for a moment, then went on carefully, "Has it ever occurred to you that things need not continue as they are?"

"I'm not sure that I understand you," Amanda said, sure that Barton must be able to hear her heart, so loudly was it beating.

"I've been thinking, of late, that it is possible that we might make of our marriage something much more than it is now," Barton said. His fingers strayed from the lace on her sleeve to the inside of Amanda's wrist.

He began to stroke the delicate skin there, tracing
small circles over the spot where her pulse throbbed.

"In—indeed?" Amanda whispered.

"We might learn to be very happy together, if only
we tried," Barton said. Absently, as if it were something he did every day, he lifted Amanda's wrist and
pressed his lips to the spot his fingers had circled.
"What do you think, my sweet?" he breathed.
"Could you bear to be a real wife to me—a wife," he
added with a smile that made Amanda tingle, "in
every sense of the word?"

"I...you..." Words failed Amanda. She felt weak
with happiness; she knew, she thought dazedly, how
Cinderella must have felt!

"I won't press you for an answer now," Barton
said. "This is something you will wish to consider, I
know." He rose from the bench.

"Bart, I don't need..." Amanda began.

"Hush," he said gently. "The last thing I should
ever wish is to rush you into a decision. Take your
time, and think on it well." He smiled. "But do not,
pray, make me wait too long!"

CHAPTER THIRTEEN

LORD BARTON'S BUTLER opened the door to find Carolyn Travers standing on the doorstep, wrapped in a voluminous brown cloak, its hood pulled well up to hide her face. Carolyn peered past him into the empty entrance hall, held her finger to her lips and motioned Dennison outside.

"Who's at home?" she asked softly.

Dennison was puzzled, but answered readily, "His lordship has gone off to Tattersall's with Mr. Wendover to look at horses. Lady Augusta is out to nuncheon, dining with a friend."

"And Lady Barton?"

"Abovestairs, in the drawing-room."

"Excellent!" Carolyn swept past the man and into the house. She crossed the entrance hall and opened the library door. "Well, come along!" she said impatiently to Dennison, who still stood outside, staring after her.

He shut the library door behind them. "It wouldn't do for you to be found here, Lady Travers," he said nervously. "Lord Barton has made it quite clear that I am not to admit you to the house."

Carolyn smiled brilliantly. "That is one command," she said, "that need not trouble you for very much longer."

"It does trouble me," Dennison grumbled. "If Lord Barton should return home unexpectedly, he'll show me the door for certain."

"Not to worry," Carolyn said, and chuckled. "This won't take long!"

"Just what is it that you want from me?" Dennison asked suspiciously.

"Why, nothing of any moment, my friend," Carolyn answered. "In truth, I've come to do you a great favour."

"And what is that?" The servant eyed Carolyn with misgivings.

"Have you not complained to me of Lady Barton's officiousness? You've often told me how much more comfortable this house was before she came, and sworn to be revenged upon her. Well, I am here to give you your chance to pay your debt to her, and in spades."

"How?"

"The details need not concern you," Carolyn said. "Your help—for which you will be generously rewarded—will take only a few moments of your time."

"I do not wish to take chances, Lady Travers," Dennison said uneasily. "It wouldn't be worth it to me to revenge myself on Lady Barton, only to be dismissed!"

"Don't be such a coward," Carolyn said scornfully. "You've only to admit Cecil Stratton to the house when he arrives and then help me with one or

two other trifling matters and the thing is done."
When Dennison still looked undecided, Carolyn added
silkily, "Do not, pray, fail me at this late date, my
man! Else I may be tempted to tell Barton exactly what
sort of servant he has in you."

Dennison paled. "You wouldn't...Lady Travers,
I...you can't...!"

She smiled triumphantly. "I knew that I might rely
on you," she said. "Never fear, my dear Dennison, a
great deal of thought has gone into this scheme, and I
promise you, it will go off without a hitch. Just
think—a modicum of effort on your part and Lady
Barton will be brought low." Carolyn laughed, her
green eyes sparkling with excitement. "So low that
tomorrow, if she were to tell his lordship that you were
stealing the silver, he would only damn her for her
impudence!"

CHAS WENDOVER WATCHED Barton stare unseeingly
at the horses parading through the show ring, and
chuckled. "What about the roan, Bart?" he asked
mischievously. "Up to my weight, do you think?"

"Undoubtedly," Barton said absently. "A fine
specimen."

"Normally, I would bow to your superior judgement in horseflesh, but I must say, I should think that
the beast's lameness would give you pause."

"Lameness? I... Damn your eyes, Chas, they'd not
show a lame horse at Tattersall's!"

"Neither are they showing a roan at the moment."

Barton grinned reluctantly. "You've caught me out,
I fear. I must confess, I wasn't paying attention."

"So I noticed," Chas said. "What's to do?"

Barton turned away from the ring. "I took your advice, you see."

"Which advice? I'm so full of wisdom that sometimes I just can't keep track of it all."

"About Amanda," Barton mumbled. "I—I suggested to her that perhaps we should start anew—make our marriage a real one."

"But that's wonderful!" Chas exclaimed. "What did she say?"

"I did not allow her to answer me," Barton confessed. "I told her that she should think the matter over."

"Reasonable enough," Chas said.

"What if she says no, Chas?" Barton turned to face his friend. "The sad fact is, I've come to care for Amanda, more than I should ever have thought possible. What if she can't—or won't—return my feelings?"

"She will," Chas said definitely. "Lady Augusta and I are convinced that..."

"You have discussed my marriage with my grandmother?" Barton asked in an awful voice.

Chas had the grace to look abashed. "Yes, but...devil take it, Bart, we're deuced fond of you—of both of you! Is that so terrible?"

"I suppose not," Barton grumbled. He paused for a moment, then looked at his friend. "What does Grandmama think?" he asked.

"Why, that Amanda is head over heels in love with you, of course," Chas said cheerfully. "In point of fact, I share her opinion—I see it on Amanda's face every time she looks at you. If you weren't such a clunch, you would have noticed it yourself!''

"Do you really believe . . . ?''

"I really do,'' Chas said solemnly. "I don't think that you have anything to worry about, truly.''

"But I do worry,'' Barton said wryly. "Ever since I asked her if . . . well, if she'd be a true wife to me, I've been able to think of nothing else. What if I've made her hate me, Chas? I've been so stubborn, and so very unkind. . . .''

"Come with me, my lad,'' Chas said firmly. "I can see that you've allowed your imagination to run away with you. It's past time someone took you in hand! I'll drive you home, share a stiff brandy with you and help you find the bottom to confront your lady bride. But after that—'' he grinned ''—after that, my friend, you are on your own!''

AMANDA REACHED the bench in the garden and sat down. She inhaled the sweet fragrance of the roses and smiled. For as long as she lived, she thought, she would regard those particular flowers as her own, for it was here, surrounded by their beauty, that Barton had asked her to be his wife, in the truest sense of the word. She carefully plucked a bloom, picked off the thorns and tucked it into her bodice; she would leave it there, she decided, to remind her of Barton until he should return for the answer to his question. How she longed to tell him of her love, and of her eagerness to make a life with him!

A tiny frown marred Amanda's smooth brow. She had decided, in the long reaches of the night, that she would tell her husband about Cecil's attempts to blackmail her. Though the thought of doing so filled her with dread, she had decided that she could not begin her new life with Barton with a secret between them. Had not her secrets already caused them both enough pain? She could only pray that Bart would understand that although Cecil was her uncle, she and he were very different sorts of people.

Amanda heard a door slam. A moment later, Cecil Stratton came rushing through the shrubbery. "Amanda!" he shrieked, wild-eyed. "You foolish girl, what have you done? Were you not content with ruining me financially? Will you not be satisfied until I am actually dead?"

Amanda stared at her uncle blankly. "What are you talking about?"

"DeValme—it's DeValme! He's called me out!"

Amanda leapt to her feet. "What?" she gasped.

"He walked up to me in the middle of my club, right out of the blue, and accused me of mistreating you. I didn't know what he meant, of course. I protested, and he informed me that you had told him all about how I had been 'tormenting' you. When I tried to defend myself, he dashed his glass of wine in my face and insisted that I name my seconds!"

"Oh, dear," Amanda said weakly.

"Is that all you can say?" Cecil cried. *"L'Ange infame* is about to put a bullet in my heart, and all you can say is 'oh, dear'?"

"I never dreamt..."

"I'm beginning to think that this was precisely your dream," Cecil said bitterly. "I think you planned that DeValme would dispose of me."

"I did no such thing!" Amanda protested. "How can you believe me capable of such infamy?"

"Well, what are you going to do about it, then?" Cecil demanded.

"I'll speak to him," Amanda said. "I'll send him a note, asking him to call on me and then I'll explain to him..."

"A note?" Cecil spluttered. "I'm due to meet him at dawn! What if he stays out all day? What if the note is misplaced? Are you willing to gamble my life on how quickly DeValme attends to his mail?"

"You're right, of course," Amanda acknowledged. "What shall I do, then?"

"Come with me right now," Cecil urged her. "We'll run DeValme to earth, and then you may tell him in person that you do not wish him to meet me." Amanda hesitated, and Cecil said falteringly, "Amanda—you cannot want him to kill me? I know that...that I have not been the best of uncles, but surely you do not wish to see me die for it?"

"Of course not," Amanda said, making up her mind. "Only let me run upstairs and get my cloak. I'll leave a note for Barton, too, lest he should be concerned to find me away from home." Amanda picked up her skirts and moved purposefully towards the house. Cecil trailed along behind her, unable to keep from smiling smugly at her retreating back. As they came into the entrance hall, Cecil winked at Dennison behind Amanda's back. When the girl had gone upstairs, Cecil moved to join the butler. "Where is Lady Travers?" he asked softly.

"In the library, sir," Dennison said. "Mr. Stratton... are you quite sure...?"

"Just see that you do exactly as Lady Travers tells you," Cecil said roughly. "Else you will be sorry, I promise you!" He heard Amanda coming down the stairs and assumed a suitably solemn expression before turning to face her.

"Dennison," Amanda said as she shrugged into her cloak, "pray give this to Lord Barton when he returns." She handed a folded note to the servant. "Tell him that I shall be back as soon as I can."

"Yes, my lady." Dennison held the front door open for Cecil Stratton and Amanda.

A moment later, the library door opened and Carolyn peeked out. "Are they gone?"

Dennison nodded. He held out the letter. "She left this," he said.

Carolyn unfolded the paper and read it as she strolled back into the library. "How sweet," she sneered. "But I do believe I can do better!" She crumpled the note and threw it on the fire, then sat down behind the desk and took up Barton's pen. "It is fortunate that I was never much given to writing *billets doux,*" she remarked as she wrote rapidly. "Barton does not know my handwriting, and I'd be willing to wager anything that he doesn't know little Amanda's, either." She re-read what she had written, blotted it, then handed the note to Dennison. "Put this in Lady Augusta's room," she commanded him.

"With any luck, it will give the old harridan an apoplexy when she reads it."

"Will that be all, Lady Travers?" Dennison asked hopefully.

"Not quite. After you've done that, I want you to bring me Barton's largest valise, then show me to Lady Barton's room. We've one last thing to do, you and I," Carolyn said. "A bit of what they call, I believe, stage dressing!"

LORD BARTON and Chas Wendover came into the house on a burst of laughter. "Now, there is a tale," Chas concluded as Dennison closed the door behind them, "that I'd share with no one but you, Bart!"

"As I already know just what a silly clunch you can be, there's no reason not to, is there?" Barton agreed, still chuckling. He handed his hat and cane to his butler. "Where are the ladies, Dennison?"

"Lady Augusta is still out, my lord," the servant said woodenly. "Lady Barton is, I believe, in her room."

Barton could not stop himself from sending a swift, apprehensive look up the stairs. Chas took him firmly by the arm and steered him into the library. "A brandy first," he said. "Then you may go and beard the lioness in her den, so to speak."

"You must think me the greatest fool in nature to be so nervous," Barton remarked gloomily as he poured out the spirits.

"Not at all," Chas said cheerfully. "I only think you a man in love."

"I am, you know," Barton said quietly. "I'm dashed if I can say how or why it happened, but there it is."

"Can anyone ever say, really?" Chas asked. "Love lighteth where it will. But the lady you love is already your wife—in that you are luckier than most, you know!"

"So I am," Barton agreed, brightening. The two men clinked glasses in a companionable toast.

They started when the library door flew open with a bang and Lady Augusta stormed into the room. "What have you done, Barton?" she cried. "What have you done?"

"Grandmama, what is it?" Barton asked, alarmed. "What's happened?"

"Read this," the elderly woman said, thrusting a letter at her grandson. "Oh, Barton, whatever did you say to that poor child?"

Barton tore open the note and read it quickly. "Amanda!" he bellowed, and raced from the room, the paper still clutched in his hand.

"What the devil . . . !" Chas exclaimed.

"She's gone, Chas," Lady Augusta said brokenly. "She's gone!"

With a muttered oath, Chas ran after Barton. He followed his friend up the stairs and along the hall to Amanda's bedchamber.

The room was in a shambles; every drawer and cupboard was pulled open, and the wardrobe stood empty. Barton looked slowly about with a dazed expression, then his face hardened. "I have my answer, I see," he said coldly.

"Will someone please tell me what the deuce is going on?" Chas asked plaintively.

"It is simplicity itself," Barton said. "Here—see for yourself. My lady wife has gone to some pains to give me an unequivocal response."

Chas took the missive and spread the crumpled paper open. "My lord," it read.

By the time you read this, I shall be gone. Your snubs and indifrence have made this house intolerable to me; I can no longer bear to endure your many crulties. I have found someone who cares for me, someone who will treat me with the kindness and induljence that I deserve.

Please do not waste your time searching for me; I will never return to a loveless sham of a marrage.

Amanda

Chas looked up. "Bart," he said slowly, "there's something havey-cavey about this."

"How very astute you are, Chas," Barton said acerbically. "Amanda has run off with God knows whom, and you deduce that there is something wrong! I salute your perspicacity."

"No, I mean that there's something . . . not quite right about this letter," Chas persisted. "Look at it, Bart—only look at it!"

"I've seen it, thank you!" Barton snapped, and turned away.

"Then listen," Chas said urgently. "It says . . ." He ran his finger along the page. "It says that Amanda can no longer tolerate your indifference.... It says that she will never return to a loveless sham of a marriage. This makes no sense, Bart. After your conversation yesterday, why should she write such a thing? She might have said that she didn't care for you, or that she had no desire to be your true wife, but not that she could no longer tolerate your indifference!''

"Can you never stop defending her, Chas?" Barton asked. Chas winced at the pain on his friend's face.

"Barton!" Lady Augusta turned away from Amanda's dressing-table. "The jewellery is gone!" Barton shrugged indifferently. "Pray use the wits that God gave you, boy," she said sharply. "Amanda was never comfortable wearing the jewels. Why should she take them with her?"

"Need I remind you how valuable they are, Grandmama?"

"Can you really think that Amanda would steal from you?" Lady Augusta stepped closer to her grandson. "Can you?"

"What else am I to believe?" Barton asked; his tone was desolate.

Chas was still examining the note. "It's a forgery, by God!" he breathed. "Look here—and here! Amanda was an assistant schoolmistress. Is it likely that she would make such errors in spelling? She never wrote this—I'd stake my life on it!" He held the paper out to Barton. "'Tis plain as a pikestaff," he said.

Barton frowned and was silent for a long moment. "Let me see that," he said finally. His friend complied, and Barton studied the missive closely. "But who else could have written it?'' he asked. ''And where is Amanda?''

''I don't know,'' Lady Augusta said grimly, ''but I've a fair notion who does!'' She tugged on the bell-pull.

Dennison entered the room so quickly that he might have been waiting in the hall outside. He looked around the dishevelled bedchamber, his expression guarded. ''Yes, my lord?'' he asked cautiously.

Barton stared at his servant, and the man paled visibly. The peer stepped closer, his eyes never leaving Dennison's face. As he continued to glare at the man, Dennison began to tremble. ''I don't know anything!'' he cried suddenly.

Barton was across the room in a flash. ''Where is she?''

Dennison licked his lips. ''My lord, I...''

''Do not, pray, attempt to spin us a tale,'' Lady Augusta said. ''Else I shall personally see to it that you spend the rest of your days in Newgate!''

''Not Newgate, ma'am,'' Chas corrected her. ''Should he lie to us, he'll never *live* to see Newgate.''

Dennison's courage deserted him. ''They made me do it,'' he whined. ''I didn't want to, I swear it. But Lady Travers, and that Mr. Stratton...''

''Cecil Stratton?'' Barton exclaimed.

''Lady Barton left with him,'' Dennison said eagerly. ''Lady Travers took all my lady's things and wrote that letter. She warned me that if I told, she'd...'' He swallowed.

''Where did they take her?'' Chas asked urgently. ''Think, man—where?''

"I don't know!" Dennison wailed. "They never told me."

Barton started for the door. "Carolyn will know," he said grimly. "And she'll tell me, too, or I'll throttle it out of her, the jade!"

"I'm coming with you, Bart," Chas said. "We can't have you committing murder! Lady Augusta, will you...?"

"I'll stay here in case Amanda should return," Lady Augusta promised. "And in the meantime..." She swung round to face Dennison. "You and I, sir, shall have a little chat!"

CHAPTER FOURTEEN

AMANDA LEANED FORWARD and peered out the hackney cab's window. Cecil had insisted on hiring a public conveyance; he had told his niece that there was no time to wait for her carriage to be prepared. "Why are we going into the country?" she asked doubtfully. "Surely we should be looking for DeValme in Town?"

"I—I just recalled, he mentioned that he was engaged to go hunting today," Cecil mumbled. He did not meet Amanda's gaze.

"How will we ever find him, then?" Amanda exclaimed, exasperated. "We can't very well go bouncing through the fields in this cab looking for him!" She raised her hand as if to rap on the roof. "We should be very much better off going back to Town and awaiting his return."

Cecil grabbed her wrist. "There's an inn," he said glibly. "DeValme will be stopping there to lunch. We should be just in time to catch him."

"I don't see..." Amanda began impatiently.

"Please, my dear? You can't imagine what it is like to have a sentence of death hanging over your head." Cecil tried to look pitiable. "I shall go mad if I am obliged to return to Town and simply wait."

"Very well," Amanda grumbled, "but I warn you, we are on a fool's errand!"

The hackney turned off the main road and onto a narrow country lane. They travelled down this bumpy track for several miles, then pulled up before a small, disreputable-looking establishment called The King's Arms.

Amanda regarded the public house doubtfully. "This doesn't seem the sort of place that DeValme would frequent, does it?"

Their destination reached, Cecil could not contain a chuckle. "DeValme has a way," he said, "of making himself at home in the most unlikely surroundings." He helped Amanda down from the cab and held a brief, low-voiced conversation with the driver. Then he escorted his niece inside.

They stepped directly into the taproom, a long, low-ceilinged chamber that smelled of sour ale. In a chair before the fire sat the Vicomte DeValme, impeccable in black frock-coat and breeches. *"Bonjour, mon vieux,"* he called, and rose to his feet. "Amanda, my dear—how good it is to see you!"

Amanda frowned. "I thought you were hunting," she said. "Cecil told me..."

"I fear that you have caught us out," DeValme responded calmly. "That was a—what is the word?— ah, yes, a taradiddle." He turned to Cecil. "You have done well, my friend. My congratulations."

"I've fulfilled my end of the bargain, DeValme," Cecil said.

"And you shall be suitably rewarded, just as I promised." The *vicomte* pulled a folded document from his pocket. "Your vowel, sir." He handed it to Cecil.

Amanda felt her heart beginning to hammer in her chest. "I don't understand," she said.

"Very simple, my pet—your uncle has, in effect, sold you to me."

Amanda drew in her breath. "You're mad!"

"Not at all." DeValme appeared to be enjoying her discomfiture. "Indeed, some might say that it was *you* who had taken leave of your senses. Did you really think that I would allow you to defy me?" As Amanda stepped back, he continued, "I was very hurt when you ran away from me, *chérie*. After all, it was not a slip on the shoulder that I offered you, but a position of honour. I had planned to make you my wife! But you scorned me, my lady." DeValme smiled, a smile that made Amanda shiver. "Now you must, I fear, pay the price—you and that arrogant husband of yours."

"What have you done to Barton?" Amanda cried. "If you have hurt him, I'll..."

"Look, Cecil," DeValme said, amused. "The young cat defending her kittens! A pretty picture, my pet, but unnecessary, I promise you. My revenge on your husband will be a deal more subtle than anything you can envision."

Amanda pressed her hands to her middle and took a deep breath. "What is it that you want from me?" she asked, striving to remain calm.

"Why, to ruin you, of course," DeValme answered cheerfully. "Regard the beauty of my scheme! I shall take you, and use you, and make certain that *tout le monde* knows that you have run from Barton's bed to mine. Picture his dismay, if you will—the young eagle will find it difficult to soar while wearing cuckold's horns, will he not? And then, when I've tired of you, I shall give you back to Barton. He may divorce you and look the fool, or keep you and look the fool. Either way, his humiliation will be complete.''

Aghast, Amanda swung round to face her uncle. ''Cecil,'' she pleaded, ''you cannot let him do this—I am your own blood! Help me, for pity's sake!''

''''Tis your own fault,'' Cecil mumbled. ''You brought it on yourself! Had you married DeValme as you ought to have...''

''You sicken me,'' Amanda hissed. ''Coward!''

''You're still dashed high in the instep, aren't you, niece?'' Cecil retorted maliciously. ''Well, we shall see how haughtily you speak after DeValme has schooled you!''

''Very edifying, I'm sure, but it is time that you left us, Cecil,'' DeValme said. ''Good evening!''

Amanda spun round to face the *vicomte* as Cecil Stratton left the hostelry. ''You are wasting your time,'' she said clearly. ''I would die before ever I'd submit to you!''

''Oh, my dear,'' he answered, ''you have no idea how much your defiance excites me! But be at ease; your virtue is safe for the moment.'' He pulled out his pocket watch and checked the time. ''We are travelling to a little hunting box that I have in the country; it will be ever so much more romantic—and private!''

''No!'' Amanda cried wildly. ''I will not go!''

"But you shall, my sweet." DeValme took Amanda's wrist in an iron grip, and began to drag her towards the door. "I promise you, you shall!"

CAROLYN TRAVERS SET the diamond-and-emerald coronet more firmly on her curls, adjusted the long strand of pearls that hung around her neck and slipped yet another bracelet onto her slender wrist. She rose and crossed to the gilt-framed mirror that hung on the wall; turning this way and that, she admired her own reflection.

Her maid stepped into the room and announced, "Cecil Stratton, my lady." She regarded her mistress with misgiving, carefully averting her eyes from the small chest, overflowing with jewellery, that stood on a side table. "Shall I tell him that you're not at home?"

"Not at all, Mavis." Carolyn was full of good humour. "See him in, see him in!"

A moment later, Cecil stepped into the room. "Good Lord!" he said faintly. He moved to the table as if drawn on a string. His eyes glittering, he reached for the chest.

Carolyn slapped his hand. "Naughty, naughty," she said mockingly. "You have had your payment, Cecil. This is mine!"

"Where did you get..." He stopped. "Are they Amanda's?"

"More or less," Carolyn said. "I dare say most of them are Barton's family heirlooms—or were!" she added with a trill of laughter.

"DeValme will not like this, Carolyn," Cecil warned. "Didn't he insist that we should follow his plan precisely?"

"Nonsense," Carolyn scoffed, tossing her head. "I deserve some reward for all my time and trouble. And little Amanda will not be needing them henceforth, will she?"

Cecil shook his head. "I don't like it, my dear," he said. "I've the awful feeling that all this may blow up in our faces."

"Don't be such a nodcock, Cecil," Carolyn said scornfully. "What could go wrong? DeValme has the girl, has he not?" Cecil nodded. "There you are, then—we've done it! What could go amiss now?"

"What if Barton is not fooled?" Cecil asked. "What if he goes after Amanda?"

"But why should he?" Carolyn retorted. "You told us yourself that he did not wish to marry her. Why should he run after her, then?"

"To avoid the very scandal that we are trying to create."

"He can have no notion of what DeValme's intentions are," Carolyn pointed out. "I'm sure he believes that Amanda has run off to the Continent with a lover and that she'll never be heard from again." She returned to the mirror and began to toy with the pearls wrapped round her throat. "It's all worked out very nicely," she said complacently. "I have no doubt that Barton will be more than happy to resume his relationship with me once he gets over the shock of being publicly cuckolded. And if he does not—" she touched the coronet lovingly "—I shall have these to console me!"

"Carolyn!" Barton's cold voice rang out. Carolyn and Cecil both spun about. Carolyn drew in a deep, shuddering breath, and Cecil turned a pasty white.

"Why...why, Barton!" Carolyn said, striving in vain to achieve a light tone. "You startled me, *chéri.*" She held out both hands. "How are you, my..." She stopped, catching sight of the bracelets that still adorned her arms, and whipped both hands behind her.

Barton crossed the room with two long strides and plucked the coronet from Carolyn's head. "Where is she, Caro?" he asked.

Across the room, Cecil began to sidle towards the door. He had almost reached it when a hand fastened on the back of his collar. "Going somewhere, Stratton?" Chas Wendover asked pleasantly.

"I, er, I can see that Lady Travers and his lordship wish to be private," Cecil stammered. "I wouldn't wish to intrude!"

"Not at all," Chas said. "I'm sure that Barton quite welcomes your presence. Don't you, Bart?"

"Neither one of you will leave here until you tell me what you have done with Amanda!" Barton said ominously.

Carolyn attempted to brazen it out. "Can't you keep track of your own wife, my dear?" she asked sweetly. "How unfortunate, to be sure."

"Do not try my patience, Caro," Barton said tightly. "If you don't know where Amanda is, then where, pray tell, did you get this?" He shook the coronet in her face.

"She gave it to me," Carolyn said, thinking rapidly. "Amanda told me that...that she was leaving you, but she said she could not bear to part with her jewels. She asked me to hold them for her."

"Can you truly think me fool enough to believe such a half-witted tale?" Barton asked scornfully. "You are the last person on Earth from whom Amanda would ask a favour!"

"How can you be so sure, *chéri?*" Carolyn taunted him. "It appears that you do not know your little bride as well as you thought. And how should you? Given the brief nature of your acquaintance..." She shrugged disdainfully.

Barton seemed to swell with rage. He took a step towards Carolyn.

"Bart, don't!" Chas called urgently.

Barton stopped and took a deep breath. "You're right, of course," he said. "No matter how richly she deserves it, I may not offer a woman violence." He swung about to face his wife's uncle. "But, you, Stratton...you are a different matter altogether!" He began to move forward threateningly.

Cecil backed away. "Don't," he squeaked. "Don't!"

"Tell me where she is," Barton ground out. "Tell me now, damn you, or I'll..." He reached for Cecil's throat.

"DeValme has her!"

Barton seemed to freeze; the angry colour that had risen to his face drained away. "DeValme?" he whispered. *"L'Ange infame?"*

"It was all his scheme—his and Carolyn's," Cecil babbled. "They planned it, not me! I didn't want to help, but they made—" He gurgled as Barton's hand closed around his throat.

"Tell me where she is," Barton said in a frighteningly quiet voice. "Where has he taken her?" He gave Cecil a shake.

"Ownsbridge!" Cecil gasped. "DeValme has a hunting box there..."

Barton threw Cecil to the ground and, without another word, turned and stalked out. Chas paused on the threshold. "If you place any value at all on your own life, Stratton, you will not be in London—or in England!—when we return." Then he, too, was gone.

DEVALME REGARDED Amanda coolly, his head resting comfortably against the squabs of his carriage as the vehicle travelled through the deepening twilight. Amanda glared back at him, then looked away.

"Still so defiant, my dear?" The amusement in DeValme's tone made Amanda clench her fists in frustration. "Why not relax and bow to the inevitable?"

"I will never give in to you—never!" Amanda spat out.

"Ah, but you will, you know," DeValme said. "You have no choice, you see! But it will not be so bad, truly." He reached out and ran his finger along Amanda's jaw. She jerked her head away. "Why not try to persuade me to be kind, *chérie?* I promise you, I respond well to sweet words."

"Barton will kill you for this!"

"I think not." DeValme leaned back in his seat. "I doubt very much that he'll even trouble himself to look for us. He did not wish to wed you in the first place, did he? And if he is foolish enough to challenge me, so much the better! I should be quite happy to oblige his lordship, and put a period to his existence."

"How can you be so wicked?" Amanda asked desperately.

"The simplest thing in nature, pet—I've had a lifetime of practice!" DeValme sneered.

The carriage jerked, then pulled to a swaying halt. "Ah," the *vicomte* said. "We've arrived."

Amanda shrank back into the corner of the carriage, but DeValme reached across and took her by the shoulder in a grip so tight that it made Amanda cry out. "Do not, pray, be tiresome, my dear." He pushed her outside. "It will do you no good whatsoever, and if you put me in a bad temper, well!" He shrugged. "You must then suffer the consequences."

The door to DeValme's hunting box was opened by an ancient, bent woman who grinned toothlessly and bowed at the sight of the *vicomte*. "Before you allow your hopes to soar, I must tell you that Marthe is a devoted family retainer, and deaf as a post into the bargain. She will neither know, nor care, what takes place here tonight." DeValme propelled Amanda through the front door and into the hall. Turning, he dropped a heavy wooden bar into place across the portal. "There, now!" he said pleasantly. "We are all snug and tight for the evening." He waved a hand at his aged servant and, with another bow, she shuffled out of sight.

He took a step towards Amanda. "DeValme... please!" she cried. "Don't..."

"My dear child," DeValme purred.

Amanda picked up her skirts and, after one desperate look about her, ran up the stairs at one end of the hall. She could hear DeValme laughing as he came up behind her; she ran down the first-floor passageway, through an open door and slammed it closed. The room was a bedchamber—the very one, Amanda realized with horror, that must have been prepared for her and DeValme! A fire burned in the grate, and the bed covers were turned back invitingly. At the end of the chamber stood a pair of French doors. Amanda raced to open them and stepped out onto a small balcony that overlooked the terrace. The branches of a tree grew near the balcony; Amanda strained, but, try as she might, she could not come close to reaching them.

"No escape that way, I fear," DeValme said. Amanda gasped, and whirled round to find him standing in the open doorway. "It would take much strength, and not a little luck, to make that leap!" He advanced into the room, his lips lifted in a smile. "What a goose you are, to be sure," he said amicably. "I was merely about to ask you to join me for an intimate supper. There was no need to take flight!"

"I'm not—" Amanda began, then stopped. "Thank you, my lord," she continued after a moment. "I am quite famished!"

DeValme's eyes gleamed. "Ah," he said. "This is what is called the delaying tactic, is it not? But no matter. It is better that you dine, my dear." He took Amanda's arm in a steely grip. "You will need your strength later!"

DeValme led Amanda downstairs and into a small dining-room that opened off the entrance hall. The room was comfortably furnished; a thick carpet lay on the floor and a heavy oak table, set for two, stood before the fireplace. The walls were decorated with mounted weapons, ranging from a fowling piece to a pair of crossed duelling swords that hung over the mantel. Amanda eyed them consideringly, but realized, chagrined, that all the pieces were set too high on the walls for her to reach.

The *vicomte* followed her gaze and chuckled appreciatively. "How very bloodthirsty you are, to be sure," he remarked. "But I shan't take it amiss. I have always preferred a woman of spirit!"

DeValme courteously held Amanda's chair for her. She sat and loaded her plate with as much of the cold chicken, fruit and cheese as it could hold. She ate very slowly. Though each mouthful threatened to choke her, she was determined to finish every bit. Her companion ate in silence; he raised his eyebrows when Amanda refilled her plate, but made no comment.

At last Amanda could not force down another bite. She slowly laid her fork beside her plate and regarded DeValme apprehensively.

"The time has come, my pet," he said, and made as if to push back his chair.

"No!" Amanda cried. "That is to say... might I trouble you for a brandy?"

DeValme hesitated, then shrugged. "Very well." He crossed to the sideboard and filled two glasses with the amber liquid. "It is likely just as well that you take a moment or two to let your meal settle," he allowed. "I'd no idea that you were such a formidable trencherwoman!"

Amanda sipped her brandy slowly, her gaze fixed yearningly on the large window behind DeValme. Then her eyes widened, and involuntarily she breathed, *"Barton!"*

DeValme chuckled. "Are you actually reduced to praying to him, *chérie?* It will do you no—"

The window shattered with a crash, and Lord Barton leapt into the room.

"Oh, Bart!" Amanda cried, and flew across the room to his side.

Her husband slipped an arm about her waist. "Are you all right, love?" he asked anxiously.

She nodded. "I'm fine. He didn't... he didn't hurt me."

Barton turned to DeValme. "Well met, *monsieur,*" he said, his voice like ice.

The *vicomte* rose, his aplomb apparently unshaken. "Barton," he acknowledged, inclining his head.

"You have a great deal to answer for, sir!" Barton was keeping a tight rein on his temper.

"But how is that?" DeValme enquired politely. "I have only taken from you that which you did not desire." He moved towards the fireplace and leaned against the mantel. "Or am I wrong? Can it be that you have developed an affection for the doxy who trapped you?"

"I say, that's enough!" Chas Wendover had climbed unnoticed through the broken window. He started towards DeValme, only to have Barton lay a restraining hand on his sleeve.

"Very good!" DeValme said approvingly. "This is between the two of us, my lord, is it not?" He turned and pulled down the duelling swords that hung above him. "Shall we settle it, then?" He tossed a weapon to Barton, who snatched it out of the air. *"En garde!"*

"Bart, no!" Amanda cried. Barton pushed his wife into Chas's arms and stepped forward to meet the *vicomte.*

Their swords flashed; the small room rang with the sound of steel meeting steel. DeValme was an excellent foilsman. He had a wrist both supple and strong, and he had been trained by French masters of the art. But it soon became evident that he had met his match in Barton. Inexorably, he was forced back by Barton's furious attack—across the dining-room, through the open door and out into the entrance hall.

"Will you yield?" Barton grunted. "I am willing to let you go with your life if you'll swear on your name never to return to England."

DeValme spat on the floor. "I will have her, *cochon,* while your dead body is cooling!" He reapplied himself to the fight with a vengeance.

Up the stairs they fought, with Amanda and Chas trailing behind. Barton pressed harder and harder, his sword a blur in the dim light of the first-floor passageway. DeValme moved ever backward; he was clearly tiring and having more and more difficulty parrying Barton's thrusts and lunges.

The two men moved across the bedchamber that had been prepared for DeValme and Amanda. Barton, catching sight of the waiting bed, paled and redoubled his attack. DeValme was forced through the open French doors and out onto the balcony.

"Prepare to die, devil!" Barton said.

"This has all been very amusing," DeValme panted, "but 'tis past time that I was gone!" He hurled his sword at Barton, jumped to the rail of the balcony and leapt, his hands reaching out for the branches of the tree.

Amanda screamed. Barton grabbed for the man, but too late; DeValme fell, missed the branches and landed with a thud on the cobbled terrace below.

"Is he . . . ?" Amanda whispered.

"I think so," Chas said soberly. "His head . . ." Chas swallowed. "He's dead."

Barton leaned on the railing, breathing heavily. "Bart . . ." Amanda took a hesitant step towards her husband. "I am so sorry!" She began to weep softly.

Her husband frowned. "That DeValme is dead?"

"No!" Amanda cried. "May God forgive me, but I'm glad of that."

Barton moved closer to his wife. "What are you sorry for, then?" he asked.

"For this!" She waved a hand. "For all the trouble I've been to you. For everything!"

Barton smiled and slipped his arms about his wife. "You have been something of a bother, I won't deny it," he said. He lifted Amanda's chin. "But if I must choose between trouble with you, or no trouble without you... well, at the very least, life will not be boring!"

Amanda searched his face. "Are you sure, Bart? Are you quite sure?"

"Are *you* sure, Amanda?" he retorted. "If you...if you stay with me, from now on we shall be man and wife, and none of this 'in name only' nonsense. Can you live with that, love?"

Amanda stared up at Barton, her throat aching with all that she felt for him. "Oh, Bart..." With her heart in her eyes, she added simply, "I don't think I could live without it!"

THREE UNFORGETTABLE HEROINES
THREE AWARD-WINNING AUTHORS

Untamed
MAVERICK HEARTS

A unique collection of historical short stories that capture the spirit of America's last frontier.

HEATHER GRAHAM POZZESSERE—over 10 million copies of her books in print worldwide
Lonesome Rider—The story of an Eastern widow and the renegade half-breed who becomes her protector.

PATRICIA POTTER—an author whose books are consistently Waldenbooks bestsellers
Against the Wind—Two people, battered by heartache, prove that love can heal all.

JOAN JOHNSTON—award-winning Western historical author with 17 books to her credit
One Simple Wish—A woman with a past discovers that dreams really do come true.

Join us for an exciting journey West with
UNTAMED
Available in July, wherever Harlequin books are sold.

MAV93

Relive the romance...
Harlequin and Silhouette
are proud to present

by Request

A program of collections of three complete novels by the most
requested authors with the most requested themes. Be sure to
look for one volume each month with three complete novels by
top name authors.

In June: **NINE MONTHS** Penny Jordan
                            Stella Cameron
                            Janice Kaiser

**Three women pregnant and alone. But a lot can
happen in nine months!**

In July: **DADDY'S**   Kristin James
           HOME   Naomi Horton
                            Mary Lynn Baxter

**Daddy's Home...and his presence is long
overdue!**

In August: **FORGOTTEN**   Barbara Kaye
           PAST   Pamela Browning
                            Nancy Martin

**Do you dare to create a future if you've forgotten
the past?**

Available at your favorite retail outlet.

HARLEQUIN®   Silhouette

REQ-G

Harlequin is proud to present our best authors and their best books. Always the best for your reading pleasure!

Throughout 1993, Harlequin will bring you exciting books by some of the top names in contemporary romance!

In July
look for
The Ties That Bind by

JAYNE ANN KRENTZ

Shannon wanted him seven days a week....

Dark, compelling, mysterious Garth Sheridan was no mere boy next door—even if he did rent the cottage beside Shannon Raine's.

She was intrigued by the hard-nosed exec, but for Shannon it was all or nothing. Either break the undeniable bonds between them . . . or tear down the barriers surrounding Garth and discover the truth.

Don't miss THE TIES THAT BIND . . .
wherever Harlequin books are sold.

Fifty red-blooded, white-hot, true-blue hunks from every State in the Union!

Beginning in May, look for MEN MADE IN AMERICA! Written by some of our most popular authors, these stories feature fifty of the strongest, sexiest men, each from a different state in the union!

Two titles available every other month at your favorite retail outlet.

In July, look for:

CALL IT DESTINY by Jayne Ann Krentz (Arizona)
ANOTHER KIND OF LOVE by Mary Lynn Baxter (Arkansas)

In September, look for:

DECEPTIONS by Annette Broadrick (California)
STORMWALKER by Dallas Schulze (Colorado)

You won't be able to resist MEN MADE IN AMERICA!

Where do you find hot Texas nights, smooth Texas charm and dangerously sexy cowboys?

Crystal Creek

AFTER THE LIGHTS GO OUT
by Barbara Kaye

Trouble's brewin'—Texas style!

Jealousy was the last thing Scott Harris expected to feel. Especially over an employee. But one of the guests at the Hole in the Wall Dude Ranch is showing interest in his ranch manager, Valerie Drayton, and Scott doesn't like it one bit. Trouble is, Val seems determined to stick to Scott's rule—no fraternizing with the boss.

CRYSTAL CREEK reverberates with the exciting rhythm of Texas. Each story features the rugged individuals who live and love in the Lone Star State. And each one ends with the same invitation...

Y'ALL COME BACK...REAL SOON!
Don't miss AFTER THE LIGHTS GO OUT
by Barbara Kaye
Available in August wherever Harlequin books are sold.

FLASH:
ROMANCE
MAKES
HISTORY!

History the Harlequin way, that is. Our books invite you to experience a past you never read about in grammar school!

Travel back in time with us, and pirates will sweep you off your feet, cowboys will capture your heart, and noblemen will lead you to intrigue and romance, *always* romance—because that's what makes each Harlequin Historical title a thrilling escape for you, four times every month. Just think of the adventures you'll have!

So pick up a Harlequin Historical novel today, and relive history in your wildest dreams....

HHPROMO